FALLING

Book #1 in the Saints of Salvation Series

By

VJ Dunn

D1282648

HEA Publishers
PO Box 591
Douglas, AZ 85608-0591
Or email: author@vjdunn.com

Table of Contents

Chapter 1 1

Chapter 2 21

Chapter 3 43

Chapter 4 63

Chapter 5 83

Chapter 6...103

Chapter 7...119

Chapter 8...137

Chapter 9...159

Chapter 10...177

Chapter 11...199

Chapter 12...221

Chapter 1

SPARKS SOARED into the night sky, a dance of fireflies caught up in a swirling wind. A hushed sound of distress escaped some of the onlookers when the roof of the church gave up its fight before the ever-present oppressive silence fell upon them once again.

They had to be silent; the enemy was listening. Always listening.

Nathan flinched when one of the building's sides collapsed outward, spilling debris and embers onto the once pristine lawn. Now that patch of grass that had been the envy of the neighborhood was parched like the rest of the landscape, untended with no one left to care for it. Flames licked at the dried blades of grass which quickly succumbed as the fire spread across the lot.

He didn't hold any particular fondness for the little white church that perched like a beacon on the corner of their street, but he wrapped his arm around his wife's shoulder when she sobbed softly, offering silent condolence. Tammy had grown up in the Baptist church and watching it crumble to the ground like a sandcastle giving in to the tide had to be difficult.

The arson was just one more crime in a very long string of them in their city. Rapes, murders, robberies... all the numbers had skyrocketed once the economy crashed, and the citizens panicked. Truthfully, though, the devastating financial situation seemed like just an excuse for the scum of the earth to crawl out of its hole.

Nathan knew their town wasn't the only place

suffering from the crash. Before he'd been unceremoniously booted from the town's police force when life handed him an unsavory platter of "sucks to be you," they'd been getting reports from all over Indiana about crime rates reaching unprecedented levels. Police in all divisions and departments were blindsided by it and no one knew what to do.

It had been expected that the governor would declare martial law and bring in the National Guard, but there was just too much chaos... and too few to deal with it. And instead of asking for volunteers to stay on and help fight against the anarchy, the police departments had just let everyone go.

Nathan was still shaking his head over that decision.

Tammy continued to sob quietly as the structure finally gave way and crumbled into a mass of twisted metal and burning timber. He tugged on his wife's hand to pull her away from the scene.

"C'mon," he murmured, "there's no reason to stay here." She nodded against his side, but then separated herself to hug some of the other onlookers. A few Nathan recognized—the pastor of the church, Ralph, for one, and his wife Eddy. The couple had been after him for years to come to church, to accept Jesus as his "savior."

Nathan wasn't having any of that nonsense.

Once his wife said her goodbyes, Nathan wrapped his warm around her shoulders and led her away. They'd been on their way out of town when Tammy saw the flames in the little church's window and had rushed toward the building. Nathan had barely managed to grab her before she'd flung the front door open. What she'd been planning to do, he had no clue.

He was just thankful that he'd been able to stop her in time.

"How far are we going?" Tammy said, barely above a whisper.

"Gerald's house," Nathan said, wincing when she sucked in a sharp breath.

"That far?"

He nodded; it was necessary that they get as far away from the city as they could, and as quickly as possible. They were already starting to lock down cities and towns of any notable size and Nathan didn't want to get stuck "inside" where there wasn't a safe place to be, nor a way to get out. At least they had a place to escape to.

When it was evident after a few chaotic months that life wasn't going to return to "normal," his friend from the police department had offered for them to stay with his family outside of the city. At the time, Nathan had secretly scoffed at Gerald's offer; he was certainly man enough to hold his own against the petty thieves and others causing general mayhem. But then everything got worse.

So much worse.

And then there was the other consideration—that Tammy would be better off with people she knew when Nathan started down that slippery slope he found himself on. Gerald was one of only three people who knew about the horror he would soon be facing. Another was his precinct supervisor.

The other was his doctor.

He shook his thoughts away as he navigated them around a giant, newly formed pothole. Nathan didn't want to tell Tammy the reason why they'd need to walk over twenty miles in the pitch-black night. It was a hazardous time to travel, with unseen dangers in their path likely to trip them, but he'd picked the moonless night for a reason. While they might not be able to see their surroundings, they in turn would not be seen.

And the new enemy was always watching. Listening and watching.

It had been whispered that they were quick to shuttle off "dissidents" to unknown places, just for voicing discontent or sharing an opinion. Nathan knew of several people who'd disappeared shortly after the enemy had shown itself. And those people had all been known to be very vocal in their conservative beliefs.

The time for having a voice of freedom had passed. They were no better off than Russia in the seventies. And soon, freedom would be as rare as it had been in Germany during the first four decades of the nineteen hundreds.

If he were a believer, Nathan supposed he'd be praying like his wife was so fond of doing. Tammy had certainly spent a good portion of her time on her knees after the economic collapse. He'd never known her to be so pious, but when everything started heading south toward the bowels of hell, she'd suddenly remembered her religion.

Nathan wished she hadn't, because his wife had started hounding him to "get right with the Lord."

He gritted his teeth at his thoughts. If there was one thing he couldn't stand, it was hypocrites. And as far as he was concerned, all Christians were just that. Nathan supposed that assumption was probably unfair, but the beliefs were embedded deep within him, like a sticker from a thistle that broke off under the skin.

It didn't help that he'd been raised in a strict Jewish home, one that lambasted the Christian faith, especially in claiming that the Jews' coveted Messiah had already come. His family had spent years drilling it into his head that "true Jews" still awaited their savior, and that the Christian's claim was "blasphemous heresy."

Truth be told, Nathan didn't really believe the Jews either. As far as he was concerned, "God" was just myth created by man to keep people in line.

He kept his thoughts to himself, though. While Tammy hadn't been practicing her religion when they'd met and married—if she had, he never would have asked her out in the first place—he didn't begrudge her for falling back on it. The times were scary and if it made her feel better to pray to a myth, then he wasn't going to say anything.

A sound to his left startled him and he reached out for his wife, inadvertently hitting something soft that made her yelp. He hissed softly, the sound telling her to be silent as they both stopped moving and just listened.

It was difficult to pick out individual sounds, what with the clamor of the night. Nathan thought that it was strange how those who weren't breaking laws and wreaking havoc were quiet, staying under the enemy's radar; yet those who were bent on crime sprees had no such qualms. They hooted and hollered and banged about, not caring who heard them. Nathan knew why they weren't afraid of the enemy.

The Neo Geo Task Force encouraged them.

Most citizens thought the newly formed "government agency" was there to provide peacekeeping, to stop the criminals from getting out of control. The "Neos," as they were called, were the good guys, the new sheriff in town. The city had breathed a collective sigh of relief when they'd rolled in.

Those in the police department knew better. The Neo Geo Task Force was no better than the S.S. of Nazi Germany. In fact, in many ways it seemed that they were worse. Far worse.

As the sounds in the night faded into the distance they continued walking, each silently considering their circumstances. Surviving was at the top of the list. Everything else paled.

Surviving had an entirely different meaning now. Before, it had been "work to make money so you can buy stuff and eat." Now, it was "Stay low, keep your head down, avoid the criminals, and above all, avoid the Neos."

All things considered, Nathan was glad the police department had let him go. Word was that the Neos were conscripting anyone who had weapons training. They'd started at the Federal level, but were now shaking down local law enforcement, looking for more minions to join their ranks. The last thing Nathan wanted to do was become another mindless Neos soldier, controlled by superiors with highly questionable ethics.

But the timing of the financial collapse couldn't have been worse. When his supervisor informed him the department would have to terminate him, Lieutenant Jeffers had also told him that he would likely be eligible for long-term disability. Nathan had been hopeful that he'd be able to stash away some money for Tammy before the inevitable happened, plus he had the life insurance policy he'd taken out when he first joined the force. With the collapse, none of it mattered because money no longer mattered.

And it terrified him to think of his wife trying to survive on her own.

Gerald had promised Nathan that he and his wife would take Tammy in, for as long as she wanted to stay. That comforted him somewhat, though he wasn't sure the offer would still stand once he was gone. Gerald had always been a good friend, but when times were as tough as they were, friendships had a way of taking a backseat to feeding your own.

A gunshot rang out and Tammy gasped, before Nathan clamped his hand over her mouth and pulled her to the shadow of a tree. Though the moonless night was dark, he didn't trust that someone might spot them. Screams filled the night then, the sound of grief, the lament over the loss of a loved one.

Nathan's heart clenched then, wondering how long Tammy would grieve over him. He hated the thought of her hurting and for the hundredth time, considered ending his life sooner than later. Get it over with. At least then she wouldn't have to watch him wither away.

He shook his thoughts aside as he concentrated on the sounds. The screams were close, in one of the nearby homes. A woman, wailing, calling "Tiffany" over and over. *Probably a child...* In his ten years on the police force, Nathan knew there was nothing worse than a child's death. He'd never met an officer who thought otherwise.

The heart-wrenching screams were abruptly cut off by another gunshot and Nathan decided to get Tammy out of the area before the shooter went on a rampage. Or before other lowlifes decided to join in on the shooting spree.

He pulled his wife along behind him as they ran

down the block toward the little back road they needed to travel down. Nathan hoped the road leading toward Gerald's farm would be deserted, as few had gasoline or the resources to get any. At least there were very few houses along the way. Less chance of running into someone with bad intentions.

They reached a cross street before he slowed down. Tammy was panting and Nathan felt a little guilty for dragging her the way he had, but it couldn't be helped. They had to get away from "civilization" as fast as they could.

Heading down the cross street, they slowed to a walk as he relaxed his guard slightly. It was a nicer neighborhood, one of Nathan's favorites. Older, but with well-kept homes and manicured lawns, it was one of the prettier areas of the town. Of course, that was true just a few months ago; nowadays, no one bothered to mow their grass or trim their shrubbery. It was just a matter of time before those nice homes were neglected and crumbling, or else taken over by the lowlifes who thought they deserved somewhere better to live.

Funny thing was, there wasn't any place that was "better." Not any longer.

Getting out of town, away from the others, was their only chance of survival. Nathan was sure of that. In the past few months, society as they'd once known it had dissolved into something entirely unrecognizable.

It was reminiscent of those ridiculous movies Nathan had seen as a kid, depicting a post-apocalyptic world where the survivors turned into savages, barbarians who held no value for human life. The survivors of the financial collapse might not be driving around in unrecognizable vehicles with bolted-on parts as makeshift armor or wearing animal skins that were little more than loincloths, but they were most certainly leaning toward savagery in every other way.

The back road they needed to be on was ten blocks away and Nathan breathed a sigh of relief as he realized they were making better time than he'd thought. Of course, some of that was due to forcing Tammy to run nearly four blocks, which he felt slightly guilty about. While he was still in good shape from his police days, Tammy had spent the past twelve years at a desk job as a dispatcher. It was how they'd met. She'd always joked about her "secretarial spread," thinking her hips were too wide. That was no longer the case as she'd lost quite a bit of weight since snacks and desserts were a luxury of the past.

Lately, they'd been lucky to eat anything at all in a day.

That was something else the Neos had promised— they had a plan to provide food for the masses. Medicine, as well. Nathan huffed a quiet laugh; there was no medicine that could help him, even if he were willing to sell his soul to the Neos devils to get it.

Food, though... that would be good to have. He really hated imposing on Gerald and his wife, but most especially since they'd be arriving without anything to offer. No food, no supplies. Nothing.

Car lights in the distance startled him out of his thoughts and he grabbed Tammy's arm, pulling her off the road and into the overgrown bushes lining the front yard of a large home. He tugged on his wife's arm, pulling her to a squat as they waited for the vehicle to drive by. Hopefully, they hadn't been spotted.

Tammy was panting again, but Nathan knew it was

due to fright rather than fatigue. "It's okay," he murmured. "I don't think they saw us." She nodded but didn't say anything.

Nathan peeked through the leaves, watching the car as it slowly approached. It seemed they were looking for something... or someone. He pulled Tammy farther into the shrubs, hoping they were out of sight.

They both released a breath when the car passed by, turning left on the street they'd just passed. Nathan stood, holding out a hand to help his wife up.

"That was close," she murmured. He nodded, though he didn't comment.

It angered him that they always had to be quiet, to keep their voices down and to be careful not to draw attention. For once, Nathan would have liked to shout, preferably from a rooftop somewhere, "Neos can kiss it!" But he supposed that was rather immature.

Tammy leaned over to dust off her knees after kneeling in the dirt. It made Nathan smile slightly, the fact that his wife was still concerned over such things. He adjusted her backpack, then shifted his own before starting to push back through the shrubs.

"Hold it right there!"

The voice startled them, though not as much as the volume. Only criminals had leave to make all the noise they wanted. The couple turned around slowly, putting their hands up.

Nathan squinted into the darkness, though he could only see the outline of the man who called out to them. He had to assume the man was armed and his heart pounded, worrying that he might shoot them with no provocation.

"We don't mean any harm—"

10

"Shut up!" the man snapped. "I don't care why you're on my property, but you've got exactly two point oh seconds to get off it!"

"Yes, sir," Nathan said as he grabbed his wife's arm and yanked her through the bushes and into the street.

"And don't you ever come back!" the man shouted.

It was then that Nathan realized he recognized the voice. It was Clyde Peters, who Nathan had helped just six months before when the old man had been robbed and left bleeding on the sidewalk in front of a diner. Nathan had driven Clyde to the hospital himself, since the man hadn't wanted to call an ambulance. He'd even waited for Clyde to get stitched up, making sure he didn't need a ride home.

Nathan paused and turned back. "Mr. Peters, it's me, Nate. Uh, Officer Diamond. You remember me, right? I was the one—"

"I don't care who you are!" the silhouetted figure shouted once again. "Get outta here!"

Nathan sighed and turned around, tugging Tammy to resume their trek away from civilization. What had once been a quiet, safe college town was now full of fearful, hateful people who only looked out for themselves. Crime was through the roof and the "peacekeepers" couldn't care less.

It was a long time later when they finally reached the end of suburbia. Nathan felt the tension in his shoulders ease, though he kept a cautious eye on the horizon, waiting for the telltale glow of the coming morning. If they didn't reach Gerald's before then, they'd have to find a place to hide until darkness fell once again.

Though they were away from the houses of the town and, more importantly, the residents who felt the need to defend what little they had left with whatever means they had at their disposal, Nathan felt more exposed on the open road. They'd only walked maybe a quarter of a mile when he couldn't get over the feeling and reached out to grab Tammy's arm.

She jumped at the contact, obviously having been lost in her own world of thought. "What's wrong?" she murmured.

"C'mon," he said a bit more loudly. There wasn't as great a need for quiet now that they were away from the town. "I... I just have a feeling that we need to get off the road." Tammy didn't answer, but she acquiesced, and they moved into the trees lining the road.

Tree branches caught at their clothing and skin as they moved through the woods. Nathan hoped they weren't deviating from their easterly path, though it was difficult to tell in the dark. He wished he'd had survival training to know how to navigate with stars, though it wouldn't have done much good with the canopy of leaves above them. Though they'd had a two-year drought and nearly every suburban lawn had long since died, it was a testament to the wild trees' survivability that they were still green.

They were no longer making good time due to the difficulty of navigating the trees in the darkness and Nathan considered moving back onto the road, feeling a bit foolish for letting nothing more than a hunch govern his actions. But when the distant rumble of a vehicle caught his attention, he realized his gut feeling had panned out.

"Get down," he told Tammy as he squatted. The rumble increased, and Nathan realized it wasn't one vehicle, but a fleet of them. And most likely Neos.

His wife made a pained sound after kneeling beside him, but she immediately quieted as they watched the approaching convoy's headlights through the trees. Nathan realized then they'd been paralleling the road nearly exactly. He also realized they were only a few dozen feet away from that road.

"Lie flat," he told Tammy as he himself stretched out on the forest floor. The crunch of sticks and leaves made him wince, though he knew that was foolish; none of the passing soldiers would be able to hear such a soft noise. He was more concerned that they would be spotted, especially since he noticed one of the vehicles toward the back of the line was shining spotlights into the woods on both sides of the two-lane road. It made him frown, wondering what they were looking for.

Or who.

Tammy's breath was coming in huffs, a clear indication she was feeling stressed. Nathan didn't blame her; his own heart was pounding like mad. If they were caught, it was likely they'd never be heard from again.

Breaking the six p.m. curfew was grounds for shooting. Of course, that punishment only seemed to be doled out to those who broke it for the "wrong" reasons—running to a neighbor's to borrow milk for a baby, or taking a loved one to the hospital. Nathan knew of two people who'd been shot dead in the street for both of those "offenses." But perversely, the criminals were given free rein on the city. It seemed there was no curfew for those up to no good.

The world was topsy-turvy.

"What's good is bad and what's bad is good,"

13

Tammy had told him when he'd shared the fact that their neighbor had been shot for trying to borrow some milk the night before. "The Bible talks about that in the end times."

Of course, Nathan had ignored her comment, since he didn't believe the Bible was actually true. As far as he was concerned, it was written by men about a make-believe god to try to scare people into acting right. The boogeyman for grownups.

The first truck in the convoy had reached the area across from where they were hidden and Nathan tensed as they drove by far too slowly for his liking. Tammy made a small sound of distress and he looked toward her, realizing he was grabbing her shoulder too tightly and released his grip. He frowned when he realized the light blue t-shirt and jeans shorts she wore might be easily spotted by the soldiers with the spotlights. Even in the darkness, he could see her clothing clearly.

"Shh," he hissed softly, reminding her to stay silent. He waited a heartbeat for the first truck to pass, then grabbed the back of his wife's shirt and tugged her. "Move farther back here," he whispered. Thankfully, she listened and scooted with him without argument, deeper into the woods.

They belly crawled into thicker brush until Nathan was satisfied they were better hidden. He made a mental note to get some neutral-colored clothing for Tammy when they got to Gerald's, since the clothes on their backs was literally all they had with them. The backpacks were reserved for what little food they could scrounge and precious bottles of water.

The convoy slowly made its way along the road, the tires of the big trucks crunching on the debris that had accumulated on the asphalt over months of disuse. Nathan estimated they were barely going five miles an hour, if that. It was obvious they were searching. That thought made him want to hold his breath.

From the headlights he'd seen, he figured there were ten trucks, and it seemed an eternity before the last truck with the spotlights passed them. As it approached, he grabbed Tammy's head and held her to the ground, a silent plea to remain still and silent. Thankfully, she understood.

They released a collective breath when the truck finally passed, but they didn't move or speak for a long time afterward, until the roar of the engines was so distant it was barely audible. Tammy was the first to break the silence.

"Thank You, Jesus. Thank You."

Nathan rolled his eyes as he released her from his near stranglehold. He didn't comment, though. The last thing he wanted to do was cause animosity between the two of them when time was so short. He didn't want her to have any bad memories of him.

"C'mon, babe," Nathan said as he pushed to a stand and grabbed Tammy's backpack, pulling her up to her knees. She gasped again, another pained sound. He frowned.

"What's wrong?"

It sounded like she was panting again, trying to get her breath. It was long moments before she spoke. "I... I have some sort of injury."

His frown deepened. "What? And how?"

Instead of standing, Tammy leaned back to sit on the forest floor. "My leg. Shin. When we first crouched down in the trees. I... I think I have a stick or something stuck in my there."

Nathan squatted beside her and squinted in the darkness, but he couldn't see anything. He regretted not bringing his flashlight, but the batteries were too drained and he didn't have any replacements. It wasn't like he could go to the store and buy any, not without any money. The last time he'd checked, two D batteries were going for twenty-five dollars. They were probably up to a hundred now. It was just a matter of time before the U.S. dollar held no value whatsoever.

He slid a hand from her ankle slowly up her leg, feeling for whatever was causing her pain. She squeaked when he touched it, while he grimaced when he realized it was a rather large chunk of wood and they had no first aid supplies with them. Nathan was starting to feel like an idiot for not thinking of all the problems they might face while traveling. He'd just been in a hurry to get out of town and hadn't planned. Not at all.

"I'm gonna have to pull it out," he murmured. "It's gonna hurt, honey, but try not to yell, 'kay?" She didn't answer, but he sensed her nodding.

"Okay, here we go, on three... one, two—" he yanked it out then and put his hand over the wound, hoping to stop any blood flow.

To her credit, Tammy made barely more than a grunt. "What happened to three?" she wheezed. Nathan smiled.

"Sometimes it's better if you're not expecting it. You woulda tensed at 'three' and it probably woulda hurt more."

Even though he held his hand over the wound, he could feel blood seeping through his fingers. Nathan started worrying about blood loss, though he was glad that her body was cleaning the wound on its own. Keeping it clean, however, was going to be a challenge. He hoped Gerald had something they could put on it.

He took off his cover shirt and ripped a strip from the bottom, then wrapped it around her leg, tying it tight enough to make her suck in a breath. "Sorry," he murmured, "gotta stop the blood flow. We'll check it in a bit and see if we can loosen it."

Nathan helped her to her feet and steadied her while she hopped. "Lean on me," he instructed her. "We're gonna have to go back on the road, cuz there's no way we're gonna be able to navigate this forest with you limping like that."

"Sorry," she muttered. Nathan leaned over and kissed her temple.

"Not like you got hurt on purpose," he told her. "And it's my fault for not packing a first aid kit."

"We didn't have one," she pointed out as they started slowly making their way toward the road. "And I can only imagine how much they cost now."

"Yeah," he agreed. "But not as much as booze. Last time I went to the store, I saw a bottle of cheap whiskey for two hundred thirty bucks. And some lady actually picked a bottle up."

A low whistle escaped his wife's lips. "People will do anything for their fix, huh?"

Nathan nodded, though she couldn't see it. "Yeah, but maybe she was buying it for medicinal purposes."

Tammy chuckled. "For pain management maybe?"

"And sterilization. You know, that's not a bad thing, now that I think of it. Maybe we oughta dump some of our water bottles out and fill them with Jack

Daniels."

Despite her need to lean on him, Tammy managed to elbow him in the ribs while laughing quietly. Nathan was glad to hear it; it had been far too long since they'd been able to find anything humorous.

It was a long while before they made it back to the road and when they cleared the trees, he had to force his panic down; the dark night was already starting to lighten. Dawn was drawing near, and they still had over eight miles to go by his estimation.

Tammy didn't make a sound as she limped and hopped alongside him while clinging to his waist. Nathan kept his arm securely around her back and had to shorten his long gait to match her shorter one. It made for a very uncomfortable walk, but he told his complaining inner voice to shut up; at least he wasn't injured like his poor wife.

They'd barely made a mile when Tammy gasped, "Nate, I have to stop." He glanced at the horizon, stifling a moan when he saw the red glow had lightened to a deep yellow. The sun was about to breach the earth and that meant they'd need to find a place to either hide or go deeper into the woods to continue their trek.

He turned them and helped her get through the trees until they found a fallen log to sit on. Tammy wheezed as she sat, and Nathan knelt in front of her. The makeshift bandage was already soaked through, and blood was trailing down her shin into her shoe. The sight made his heart lurch; the injury was worse than he'd originally thought.

Since he could see a bit better with the approaching dawn, he untied the bandage and peeled the fabric away from her wound. The sight that met him made his stomach churn; not because of the sight of blood, but because of the size of the hole in her leg. He would be able to fit his little finger into it.

Nathan was torn; instinct told him to drag Tammy into the thickest brush he could find and wait until dark to head out once again. But he knew that her wound needed tending to, and soon—it was still bleeding, and the deep puncture would likely get infected if they didn't get it treated. He swallowed hard several times, his throat working against emotion and stress.

He was running worst-case scenarios through his head, a jumble of what-ifs and what-thens, when Tammy reached out and put a hand on his shoulder. She then said the words he most dreaded to hear.

"Honey, let's pray."

Chapter 2

TAMMY KNEW that Nathan hated it when she prayed, but she felt led to do so, regardless of how uncomfortable it might make her husband. *In fact,* she thought to herself, *maybe it's BECAUSE it makes him so uncomfortable that I want to pray with him.* It wasn't a perverse thought, but one born of a need to share Jesus with him as much as possible.

He sure didn't make it easy.

She didn't give him time to protest but leaned over and grabbed his hand. "Father, thank You for keeping us safe so far. Thank You for taking care of us and for leading us on the path You're showing to us. We ask that You continue to provide and protect.

"But now, Jesus, I have a problem with my leg. This wound won't stop bleeding and we still have a long way to walk. I know my husband is worried about it and doesn't know what we should do now. Please heal my leg and lead us once more. Show us if we should stop for the day, or if we should go on to Gerald's. Thank You, Father. Amen." She sighed, suddenly very tired, and closed her eyes as she leaned against her backpack.

Tammy didn't expect an answer to her prayer. After all, she'd walked away from her faith for so long and had just recently started praying again, seeking God, asking for His forgiveness for choosing to leave Him.

While she knew that He certainly could answer her prayer for healing, she just wasn't sure if He would.

It was funny—when the economy had crashed

globally, she'd found herself seeking the God she had known growing up. But truthfully, she still had a lot of doubts. Nothing was happening like she thought it would, like she'd been taught.

The main cause of her doubt was the question of what happened to the rapture. She'd always heard about how Christians would be taken off the earth before the Tribulation started. It was taught with great conviction from the pulpit of the little Baptist church that she'd grown up in, the one she'd had to watch burn to the ground just hours before. And when the rapture didn't happen like she thought it would... the doubts started.

At first, she thought she'd been left behind, that because she'd backslid so far she was no longer one of God's kids and He'd taken only the "true" Christians with Him. Not that she'd blame God for leaving her; after all, she'd fallen into so much sin and had even married outside of her faith. To an atheist, of all things. So, it would have been no shock to discover that she'd been overlooked when the rapture happened.

But then she realized that all the believers she knew were still on earth with their feet firmly planted.

For now... Tammy was holding out for the possibility of a "mid-Trib" rapture, since the "pre" obviously wasn't going to happen. Anything was better than trying to survive the whole Tribulation. But she also knew that the Lord would provide if they did have to suffer through the whole thing. He always did.

Once she started praying again, and had humbly and sincerely asked for forgiveness, she'd started to feel stronger. Less fearful. She was just sad that she didn't have a Bible any longer. And no way to buy one, if the stores were still allowed to sell them, which she knew they weren't.

A daily dose of scripture would have done wonders to rebuild her faith.

But then the Neo Geo Task Force arrived in their mid-sized town. Tammy had taken one look at the symbol of their organization and had known that Satan was on the scene. Three jagged-looking sixes in a circle. The mark of the beast.

And her fear returned.

Though she'd been wondering why the rapture hadn't happened as she'd been taught, she still managed to cling to her faith. Others didn't though. Many people she knew to be devout believers had fallen away, assuming that because they weren't "taken up," then everything else they'd believed was a lie.

Including Jesus Himself.

Tammy shuddered. Not once in all her time of backsliding had she ever denied the truth of the Lord. She may not have been following Him—and most certainly had grieved His Holy Spirit with her actions—but she knew He was real. She'd just chosen to look away from Him.

I'm sorry... she started to pray, but stopped suddenly as a warm, contented feeling washed over her, one that could only be described as peaceful. It was like a warm, extra soft blanket on a cold winter night.

"As far as the east is from the west, so far have I removed your transgressions from you."

Tammy gasped as she opened her eyes when she heard a voice—*no, THE Voice!*—in her head. She knew then that the Lord Himself had spoken to her and tears sprang to her eyes.

"What's the matter?" Nate asked her quietly, obviously still concerned about Neos being in the area. She smiled at him and put a hand on his cheek. He may not be a believer, but Tammy loved him dearly. And she was praying for his salvation all the time. He didn't stand a chance.

"The Lord just spoke to me," she breathed, her voice betraying her wonder. It was the first time she'd ever heard an audible voice like that, one that she knew was the Lord. Pastor Ralph said the Lord didn't speak to believers like that any longer, but instead used others and His Word to speak to them. Tammy knew in that moment that he had been wrong.

She wondered what else he'd been wrong about.

As expected, Nate rolled his eyes at her declaration. But true to his respectful ways, he didn't argue with her.

"Huh," he said, the tone disbelieving. "So, how long does this prayer thing take?" he asked as he looked back down at her leg. When his eyes widened, Tammy bent over to see what had caught his attention. When she saw it, she laughed.

"Apparently not long at all," she grinned. Her wound had stopped bleeding and she realized then that the pain had eased as well. She stuck it out to the side, twisting it back and forth, then looked up.

"Thank You, Jesus! That was a really fast answer!" Nate made a sound that bordered on disgust.

"Do you want to walk some more, or do you think we should stop for the day?" Tammy asked before he had a chance to make a comment that she wouldn't like. He'd been really good so far when she'd started sharing her faith with him, but she sensed he was on the edge of losing his patience.

Her husband looked over her shoulder toward the rising sun at her back, but she knew he couldn't see it, not through the thick trees. Tammy could practically see his mind working, knowing that Nate was running through all the possibilities of what might happen one way or another. She wanted to tell him that they could rely on God to get them to Gerald's safely, but she stayed quiet. He'd probably had enough "God talk" for one day.

It was then she noticed a tremor in his cheek, a slight twitch, though it was rhythmic. It wasn't anything too unusual, certainly nothing to be alarmed about. But she had noticed other muscle twitches that Nate had recently acquired, and sometimes he dragged his right foot slightly. She considered asking him about it, asking if he was feeling all right, but then she figured that he was probably just suffering from the stress of their situation. They both were.

He glanced at her then. "If your leg is feeling better, I guess we can walk for a little bit. The woods thin out about three miles down the road, so we'll have to find a place to hole up until it's dark again."

Tammy nodded and stood, carefully lowering her weight onto her leg. But there was no pain at all, and she grinned again as she looked up at Nate.

"God is good," she said as she took a step. "No wonder they called Jesus 'the Great Physician'." He grunted again, another non-committal sound.

They walked in silence again, though Tammy thought it was silly; they were in the middle of nowhere and there wasn't any way the Neos could be listening. But Nate was particularly paranoid when it came to the group that Tammy was certain was the "new world order" the Bible talked about.

She knew there were a lot more verses that spoke of what would happen during the Tribulation, and about how bad things would get. It was pretty terrifying, truthfully, to realize that they might have to go through it all.

Keep me faithful, Father. Don't let me backslide again.

She was startled out of her thoughts when a distant sound caught their attention, the low hum of an engine. Nate grabbed her arm and pulled her under a thick tree, then used his body to push her against the trunk.

"What are you doing?" she asked in protest as the tree bark dug painfully into her back.

"Shh," he hissed. "Your clothes and backpack are easy to spot," he murmured close to her ear. "There isn't anything blue in the woods."

Tammy winced. She hadn't thought about the colors she'd chosen; she'd just chosen the most comfortable things she had, since they couldn't take clothes with them. She realized it would have been smarter to wear woods-colored clothing, something camouflage like the hunters wore. But having been a city girl all her life, she really hadn't thought such things. Nate was a city boy as well, though he seemed to be more on the ball about what they were going through.

Regardless, they were both going to have a hard lesson in survival, she knew.

The engine's hum drew closer, and Nate pressed on her even harder. Tammy wanted to poke him in the ribs to get him to back off, but she knew he was just being protective. It was one of the things she'd loved most about him when they'd met, the instinct to watch out for others. She'd never really had that in her life, certainly not from any male. Her own father would have rather she'd not been born, though he put on a very good "church face" for the congregation, since he'd been the head deacon and all.

If only that little church had known what went on behind the scenes. Tammy figured it was probably best they didn't. The shock of what one of their leaders was truly like would have been too much for most of the congregants.

Tammy closed her eyes against the harsh memories, reminding herself that it was in the past. She knew that she needed to forgive her father, too, as much as she truly didn't want to. It was something the Lord had been working on with her, laying on her heart. And it was the reason she'd strayed away from her faith.

Some things were just too difficult to face.

After a few long moments, Tammy realized that the engine they heard was from a plane that seemed to be circling the area, which made sense of why her husband was shoving her into the tree's trunk. She wondered if there was going to be a "Tammy-shaped" dent in the poor thing.

The plane moved directly over their hiding spot and they both looked up, though they couldn't see anything. Tammy figured that meant whoever was in the plane wouldn't be able to see them either and she wiggled, trying to get Nate to move back a little, to give her some breathing room.

He pushed on her even harder.

Though it was extremely uncomfortable, Tammy could feel her husband's body trembling against her. She reached out to run a hand down his arm, to offer what comfort she could. He leaned close.

"Don't move!" he whispered urgently.

Tammy wanted to roll her eyes at his overboard paranoia, but she decided to try to be understanding instead. Like her, Nate was faced with a lot of unknowns. The Neos had moved in and taken over, putting the entire town under a curfew and their watchful eye. The police had been disbanded right after and crime skyrocketed, despite the Neos' presence. Or maybe because of it. She still thought the Neos were evil, run by Satan himself.

Thanks to having worked in Dispatch, she still had contacts and knew that Nate had been let go from the department weeks before the entire police force had been officially terminated by the new government, but he'd never once told her, never said why. Tammy had waited patiently for her husband to explain, but he remained close-lipped. He'd even left every day like he was going on shift, leaving her wondering what in the world he was doing for eight hours.

None of it mattered any longer, she supposed. But it still hurt that her husband hadn't trusted her enough to tell her that he'd been fired from his job. A million different scenarios about why had run through her mind the past few weeks, and none of them were good. Some were particularly awful, and even though they were unwanted imaginings, they were also a reminder that the man she was married to was most definitely "of the world."

The hum of the engine faded after a few moments, but it was a long while before Nate eased off of her and stepped back. He ran a shaking hand over his face, then seemed to realize he was trembling and quickly tucked his hand into his shorts pocket. He glanced at her and Tammy quickly looked away, pretending to dust herself off. She didn't want Nate to be embarrassed about being frightened. Her husband was far too prideful.

He sighed. "I think we should just lay low until tonight," he murmured. She nodded, already knowing that would have been his preference after the "scare" they just had. Truth be told, Tammy wasn't really sure why they had to hide. She figured the curfews didn't apply once you were out of the city and, besides, why in the world would the Neos be looking for just two people? It wasn't like they'd committed some crime.

Nate led them deeper into the woods and Tammy worried about getting lost, but then she wanted to laugh to herself; it wasn't like they had a real destination in mind. Gerald and Felicia's wasn't the objective, just a stopping point. But then she had no idea where they were heading. Nate had just told her the day before to get ready to leave immediately and she knew that he had information he was once again withholding.

Her husband could be a difficult man.

Still, she hadn't argued or even questioned him. She was just as eager to leave the town that had been her home for her entire life years. Until just months before, she'd loved the beautiful place and had never even considered leaving. That was before the Neos, of course.

Their arrival had changed everything.

The woods grew dense as they headed in what she thought was a northern direction. She could feel blood trickling down her arms and legs from the scratches she was receiving as they made their way through the undergrowth, though she tried hard to ignore it.

Tammy knew the area was ripe for a forest fire, especially after the two-year drought they'd gone through. It was a wonder it hadn't already burned.

Nate picked his way through the vegetation, holding the larger branches for her to pass through. When she stumbled over a small fallen tree, he grabbed her by the elbow to steady her. She frowned when she felt the tremor in his hand. Surely, he wasn't still frightened.

It was several more moments before Nate seemed satisfied with the area. The tree canopy was so dense, even the morning sun wasn't able to pass through. It was a somewhat eerie atmosphere, but Tammy thought it was also cozy. There were even a few rocks that were high enough and flat enough to perch on.

She peeled her backpack off and sat on one of the rocks to loosen her shoelaces. After falling on that stick earlier, she didn't want to go barefoot and take the chance of another injury, but her feet felt hot and swollen. She certainly wasn't used to walking as much as they had.

Laughing to herself as she loosened her second shoe, Tammy thought about the fact that she had rarely walked farther than the house to her car, or the office. Having a desk job as a dispatcher certainly hadn't helped her lack of exercise.

But now that there wasn't any money for gas—or any gas available, for that matter—exercising came naturally when you had to walk everywhere. As she pulled her shoe and sock off to wiggle her sore toes, Tammy grimaced at the dirty line above where her sock had been. She understood then why Jesus talked about washing feet after traveling. If she'd been wearing sandals, her feet would be filthy.

She watched as Nate sat on the forest floor, the leaves crunching beneath him. He, too, loosened the laces of his boots, but left them on. She noticed his hand was still trembling but frowned when she realized it was just his right hand and not the left as well.

A question formed in her mind—if it were fright or stress causing the trembling, wouldn't it be both hands? She thought about asking him about it, but knew he would dismiss it with some lame excuse.

Another frustrating thing about her husband was his lack of communication.

She picked her backpack up and unzipped it, pulling out a small bag of stale nuts. They'd taken every scrap of food they had left in the house, including some of the military-type meals that Nate had bought from one of his friends at the police department. The man had been stocking up "in case of emergency," and had purchased more than he could store.

All the water bottles were warm, but Tammy figured liquid of any temperature would be welcomed by her tired body, so she took a healthy swig.

"Drink slowly," Nate murmured. "We have to conserve it." Tammy frowned at him like a petulant child, but she nodded. They only had six bottles between the two of them, so she supposed his admonition was reasonable. But she wondered why it was necessary to conserve if they were going to reach Gerald's within a day.

She handed the water to Nate, then opened the nuts and took a few out. Though the flavor was off due to the staleness, she savored the salt. They'd mostly walked in the dead of night, but it was still hot and humid, and she felt like she'd sweated all the salt out of her body.

After eating a few more nuts, she handed the pack to Nate. She could have eaten the whole pack, along with the jerky and even one of the MRE packages, but she knew that they also had to conserve their food. They had no idea what they'd find when they reached Gerald and Felicia's house, so it was wise to be conservative with the food as well.

Once their minuscule meal was finished, Tammy put the trash into her backpack, knowing it was just out of habit. She realized it was rather stupid to worry about such things since the entire earth was on the verge of imploding, but some things were deeply ingrained.

An unwanted memory from her childhood flitted through her mind. She flinched as if the beating she'd received that day was happening in that very moment. One little gum wrapper dropped to the ground by a five-year-old had resulted in both physical and emotional scars she'd likely carry all her life.

Father, I need Your help in forgiving my earthly father. I just... I don't know how. I don't even know where to begin. Help me.

"We need to get some sleep while we can," Nate said, interrupting her prayer. She opened her eyes and nodded, then slid off the rock, sitting on the ground. Surprisingly, it wasn't as hard as she thought it was going to be but realized that was due to all the forest debris that had accumulated over the years.

Emptying her backpack of the hard water bottles, she then placed it against the rock and leaned back. It certainly wasn't comfortable, but she was tired enough that she drifted quickly off. *I'm gonna sleep all day...*

"TAMMY, WAKE UP!" The words hissed at her made her want to slap them away, but Tammy managed to blink a few times, trying to get her bearings. Nate was shoving her water bottles into his backpack, and she rubbed her eyes in confusion.

"What's—" She stopped when he made a slashing motion with his hand, the unspoken command to be quiet. She looked around the area but didn't see anything and wondered if Nate was just being paranoid once again.

Instead of questioning him, though, she pushed away from the rock and moved to her hands and knees, then forced her aching body to a stand while grabbing her backpack off the ground. It was covered in leaves and she started to dust it off, but Nate grabbed her hand, hauling her behind the rocks. He motioned to her to squat down, and from her crouch she watched as he threw some leaves from under a bush onto the area where they'd been sitting. She realized he was covering up the evidence that they'd been there.

That's weird...

And that's when she heard what had caused her husband alarm. Another engine hum could be heard in the near area, but this time it sounded like motorcycles, and a lot of them. Of course, she knew it would have to be dirt bikes or ATVs to travel through the thick woods, but regardless—there were a handful of them, and they seemed to be coming their way.

Nate quickly joined her, and they flattened themselves behind the rocks. It wasn't the ideal hiding place, but with a sloping hill behind them, it was unlikely anything motorized would come from that direction.

Tammy felt like her heart was going to pound out of her chest and she grabbed Nate's hand, squeezing it for comfort. He squeezed back, but she found it didn't reassure her, not at all. They were totally defenseless.

The riders drew closer and closer, and Tammy squeezed her eyes shut, like that would somehow hide her further. Without Nate's assistance that time, she pressed her body against the rock, trying to become one with the hard surface. She felt her husband doing the same next to her.

She felt something tickling her leg and she opened her eyes to glance down, sucking in a breath when she saw a small brown spider crawling along her calf. Tammy had intense arachnophobia, but as much as she feared the eight-legged creepy crawlies, she didn't fear them as much as she did the Neos, so she slammed her eyes shut again and tried hard to ignore the bug.

Don't crawl up my leg. Don't crawl up my leg, she chanted to herself. She wasn't sure what she'd do if the creature made its way under the hem of her shorts. Probably shoot straight up into one of the trees above. Instead of waiting for that to happen, she let go of Nate's hand and brushed the creature off.

Judging by the sound, the bikes were within just a few dozen feet from where they hid. Nate blew out a slow breath, like he was trying to calm himself. Tammy could certainly understand that; she felt like she was about to faint from stress.

"Be still and know that I am God..."

She startled enough that Nate shifted beside her, a

34

silent admonition. Tammy grinned to herself. *Thanks, Dad.*

With the "peace that passes all understanding" surrounding her, Tammy relaxed and just waited for the trouble to pass. While she didn't know if the Lord would rescue her from the situation, she knew that He would be with her the whole time, no matter what she had to go through. There was an immense feeling of surrender to that. And relief.

It was clear that the bikes—or whatever they were—stopped on the other side of their hiding place, just feet away. Tammy could feel the tension coming off Nate; he was so stiff, she thought he could easily break in half. She reached out again to grab his hand, then leaned close to him, whispering in his ear, so low that only he and God could hear.

"Father, if these people are a threat to us, make us invisible. Don't let them see or hear us. Just as You passed through the crowd of Your own enemies, let us escape. Amen."

Nate made a sound, more a quick breath through his nose, but Tammy knew he wouldn't say anything, or even move to shake his head in denial. She squeezed his hand in reassurance.

"God will protect us," she murmured. Though her voice was low, she wondered if it was loud enough that the people could hear her even over the rumble of their idling motors. Nate sucked in a breath, one that sounded irritated... or terrified. Probably because she was making noise. Truthfully, she wished she could stand up and do a jig around the rock, singing, "You can't see me, you can't see me," in a taunting voice. She prayed silently that her faith would grow to such an extreme one day.

"You shall not put the Lord your God to the test..."

Oops, sorry, Father.

"They have to be here somewhere," a male voice said. It sounded muffled, and Tammy assumed he was wearing a helmet.

"Yeah," another voice agreed. "Air Watch said this was the area. But it's gonna be hard to find just two people in this jungle."

Tammy's eyes widened; Nate had been right—the plane had apparently been searching for them. Why, she had no idea. Her husband tensed again, squeezing her hand so much it was painful. She wiggled her fingers, a silent bid to relax his grip a bit.

"Well, we have twenty miles to cover," the first voice said. "Better get on with it. There's no sign of them here." With that, the motors revved and trailed off into the woods again.

It was several minutes before Nate released her hand and let out a breath he'd apparently been holding. "That was close," he murmured. Tammy smiled at him and patted his back.

"Yeah, but the Lord had our backs. Never doubt His ability to save and protect." Nate rolled his eyes but didn't comment. Tammy chuckled to herself as they stood and dusted the forest floor from their knees.

Lord, this is one stubborn man You created. It's all up to You to break through that heart of stone.

Since the searchers had already covered the area, Nate decided it was safe to stay where they were until dark. "It's not like they're gonna backtrack," he said. "Hopefully, anyway," he added with a sigh.

Tammy watched her husband. He was a bundle of nerves, twitching more violently than he had before. His right hand was shaking so badly that he fisted it and put it on his thigh, as if to hide it from her. It didn't help; even his fist was shaking. She was starting to get very worried about the man.

"Nate, are you okay?" she asked, then motioned toward his fist. "I mean, your hand—"

"Get some sleep," he interrupted, then shifted against the rock he leaned on to effectively put his back to her. Tammy scrunched her mouth to the side; Nate's ability to be uncommunicative was unmatched. *Stubborn, prideful jerk,* she thought, then grimaced.

Sorry again, Lord, for my unkind thoughts.

She sighed, but then settled against her own rock and closed her eyes once again. Knowing that the Lord was watching over them made it easy to drift off to sleep once again.

IT WAS FULLY dark before Nate decided it was safe for them to travel once again. As the night before, it was a moonless night and they both tripped and stumbled through the pitch-black woods as they tried to make their way back toward the road. Tammy knew that Nate would want to stay hidden in the foliage as they trekked, but once the road was in sight, she was going to insist they walk on firm, non-trippy ground. She was tired of getting banged up and scratched.

After what seemed like hours, the trees finally started to thin a bit, indicating they'd neared the clearing for the two-lane. Tammy heaved a sigh of relief.

"I'm walking on the road," she said, the first words

she'd spoken in hours. Nate got so tense every time she talked, as if her soft voice somehow carried across the miles to whoever was listening, that it wasn't worth trying to strike up a conversation.

"We need to stay—"

"I'm walking on the road," she repeated in a voice that said she wasn't going to argue about it. "I'm tired of tripping and being beat up by the forest. *I'm* walking on the road."

He huffed out a sigh, a long-suffering sound that made Tammy want to laugh as she continued tumbling and tripping. Thankfully it was just a few moments later when the forest floor started to gently slope upward, and she knew that the road was just a few feet away, though it was nearly impossible to tell where anything was.

"It's so dark, we'll be able to see headlights coming all the way from Ohio," she quipped.

She tripped a few more times before reaching the solid foundation of asphalt. If memory served her right, the particular road they were on wasn't maintained by the county since it was a country road, and she knew they'd still need to be careful walking. The last thing they needed was to fall into a pothole and break an ankle or something, lying helplessly, like roadkill.

The thought of night critters entered her mind then. As with spiders, Tammy had always had a rather unreasonable fear of mountain lions and bears. The statistics were such that she knew she had a far better chance of being killed by a cow, but she never could shake the fear of being mauled. At least cows didn't have sharp teeth and claws.

But it was a funny thing; once the Neos came on

the scene, it was like all the animals sort of disappeared. There was the occasional dog or cat seen in someone's window or yard, but the birds seemed to have fled, along with squirrels, foxes, rabbits and the like. In fact, she thought that spider that had been crawling on her leg was the first insect she'd seen in months, though she couldn't be sure.

She considered that, about the implications. The animals were smart enough to flee from the evil presence that had invaded, yet most of the humans weren't. As far as Tammy knew, she and Nate were the only people who'd left the town. Most of the residents seemed perfectly happy to have the "new government" take over, to make all the decisions for them. She knew it was because of the illusion of having peace, but the crime hadn't eased one bit with the arrival of the Neos. If anything, the violence seemed to have increased.

They walked once again in silence for a long while before Nate murmured, "We're here." Tammy startled at the sound of his voice and looked up to see that he'd stopped. She squinted into the darkness and saw that her husband was standing near a narrow clearing. There was some sort of sign behind him, and as she moved closer, she realized it was a mailbox. It must have been the road to Gerald and Felicia's, she thought as she breathed a sigh of relief.

Their steps seemed lighter as they walked down the dirt road leading to their friends' house. Tammy was practically giddy with the visions filling her head once they arrived—a shower, some food, and using a toilet that didn't consist of bark or stone. She was tired of doing her business in the wilderness, even though it had only been three times so far on their trip.

If her memory served, the Bonavita's house was

about a mile off the road, but they made good time with relief and expectancy urging them on. A pale glow on the horizon to their right indicated the moon had started to rise and it wasn't long before she could make out the shapes of trees, bushes and even a tractor. Moments later, the big two-story came into view.

As expected for the middle of the night, the house was completely dark. Tammy wondered if they still had electricity, though she doubted it. Utility companies were charging crazy prices for "luxuries" like electricity, gas and running water and most people had to put food first. But, living remotely as Gerald and Felicia did, she wondered if they had solar power. She sure hoped so.

Nate took the porch steps two at a time and reached out to push the doorbell button. Tammy walked up behind him.

"I don't think it's working," she said. "Probably no electricity?" He laughed slightly.

"Yeah." He glanced over his shoulder at her. "Guess I'll have to knock."

Tammy smirked. "Since it's oh-dark-thirty, you'll probably have to pound."

He started with a few knocks, which went unanswered. He then resorted to pounding, as she'd suggested. But no lights came on, and no sounds were heard in the house. Nate sighed and ran a hand over the back of his neck.

"I don't know what to do now."

Tammy stepped next to him and reached for the doorknob. It turned easily and she looked up at her husband. "There, problem solved."

Nate looked horrified. "That's breaking and..." His voice trailed off, then he gave an embarrassed laugh and shrugged. "I guess if there were still laws in place, this would be illegal, but... whatever." He then moved in front of her and walked into the house.

The place was silent; not even the hum of an appliance could be heard, leading Tammy to believe they didn't have solar power after all. The hope of a shower left her then and she felt deflated but decided to look on the bright side—at least they could possibly sleep in a real bed and not against a hard rock. Even a sofa would do.

Nate walked toward the stairs. "I'll go see if they're asleep. Bedroom's upstairs," he told her. Tammy nodded and turned toward the kitchen. She told herself that she wasn't going to be nosy, that whatever was in the cabinets didn't belong to them, but at the same time she wanted to see how the Bonavita's fared with food stores. If they had very little, then she and Nate wouldn't impose.

The first cabinet contained dishes. The second, glasses and cups. Then pots, pans, cleaners... all the things you'd expect to find in a kitchen. Everything but food. She released a defeated sigh, resigning herself to continue living on stale nuts and beef jerky.

There were some wooden stools along a counter, so she pulled one out and sat, then peeled her backpack off and dropped it on the floor next to her. It was just moments later when Nate came into the kitchen.

"No one's here," he said, sounding perplexed. "Gerald told me just two weeks ago to come out here whenever the time came to get away from the town." He shrugged. "I can't imagine what happened."

Tammy's eyes widened. "You don't think the Neos

conscripted him, do you?" The group had taken to forcing former law enforcement to serve them, and much of the time it was completely unwanted and involuntary. It was one of the reasons she was glad Nate wasn't with the force any longer.

He shook his head as he rubbed a shaking hand over the back of his neck once more. "No, I don't think so. They'd just started rounding up the officers still in town and since Gerald lives so far out, I would think he'd be last on the list." He sighed as he looked around. "Well, at least we can stay here for a while. Maybe they'll come back."

Tammy nodded, though she thought about the fact that they wouldn't be able to stay there long, not with as little food as they carried. The MREs wouldn't last long, not once they were opened, and their supply of nuts and jerky was sadly lacking. She figured they could survive maybe a week on what they had, though she also knew that a human could live for months without food.

She hoped it didn't come to that.

Father, I have to keep asking for Your help, but we're so lost here. We need food. Water. Medical supplies. You know what all we need, better than I do. So, please, would You just supply our needs, as Your Word says? She was going to say "amen," but then another thought occurred to her.

And a Bible. Please provide a Bible for me. And please get a hold on Nate. Amen.

She opened her eyes and smiled slightly, feeling the peace once again. It was in that moment that the moon rose enough that a soft glow filtered through the kitchen window. Tammy looked around the area, noticing at the things she hadn't seen before in the dark... including a note taped to a door in the corner.

Frowning, she got up and moved around the corner to cross the kitchen. She pulled the paper off the door, then moved closer to the window to read it. She laughed.

"What?" Nate asked from where he still stood in the middle of the kitchen. She waved the paper at him.

"I think God just answered another one of my prayers."

Chapter 3

I T SAYS THE combination is the 'last time we had lunch'," Tammy read to Nathan as they stood before the door in the corner of the kitchen. At first, he'd thought it was a pantry, with one set of empty shelves. But, in looking a little closer, he noticed a tiny latch under one of the shelves. The shelves swung out, revealing a very sturdy looking metal door set in a metal frame, complete with a spin dial lock that the old type of vaults had.

"Gerald must have installed this before the economy crashed," he told her. "Apparently, he realized there might come a time when the power would be out," he said, motioning to the lock.

"What's the combination?" she asked. "Do you know?"

Nathan looked at the vault door as he rubbed his neck. The tremor in his hand was getting worse and he was fairly certain Tammy had noticed it. He'd been afraid she was going to ask him about it when they'd been in the woods, but he'd managed to divert her. It was a good thing she wasn't a pushy woman, and knew she'd wait until he was ready to tell her what was going on. Just another thing he loved about her.

He forced his thoughts to Gerald and thought back through their years of friendship. They'd gone to high school together, joined the police force together, and even had the same shifts. And every single Wednesday without fail, they'd meet at their favorite diner for lunch. Nathan would order a burger and rings, and

Gerald would order whatever the special of the day was.

The last time they'd been able to have lunch was over six months before, just prior to the economy tanking and the world losing its mind. He figured the date was important, probably the combination itself, but couldn't remember when it had been.

He shared his thoughts with Tammy, who frowned as she chewed on her lip, a sure sign she was trying to remember as well. Finally, she shrugged.

"It had to be January," she said. "Or December." She glanced around the kitchen. "Maybe there's a calendar here somewhere." Nathan nodded, though he doubted it would do them any good. They could stare at dates until their eyes crossed, but it wasn't going to reveal when he and Gerald last met for lunch.

Tammy moved around the kitchen, opening drawers and cabinets, then wandered into the front room. It was just a few moments later when she returned with what he assumed was a calendar. She walked up to him, and he chuckled when he saw that it was "puppies and kitties." Felicia's doing, no doubt.

She flipped through the pages—pausing every few to "ahh" over some cute creature—then laughed.

"Every Wednesday says 'Lunch'," she told him, "like he needed to be reminded. Did Ger suffer from CRS?" Nathan looked at her in question. "As in, Can't Remember Stuff'," she added with a grin.

He laughed as he shook his head. "I have a feeling he added those 'reminders'," he said with air quotes, "after the fact. To keep anyone else from figuring out what the date was." He put his hand out. "Can I see it?" She handed the calendar to him, and he held it up to his face, squinting in the dim light.

The "reminders" were nothing special, but when he flipped the calendar to January, there was an additional notation on the second Wednesday that gave him pause.

"This one says 'Lunch' and under that it says, 'movie night—Marilyn M chick flick'."

Nathan had a hunch that was a clue, but he had no idea what it meant. "Marilyn Manson?" he asked, confused.

Tammy laughed. "It's probably 'Marilyn Monroe'. I doubt Marilyn Manson has made any movies. Not any that anyone would want to see, anyway, and definitely not chick flicks," she mumbled as she thought. "I saw some DVDs in the living room. Let's see if there's a clue in there."

There was a cabinet with a huge display of DVDs, so many that Nathan knew it was going to take hours to go through them all. To the right of the cabinet was a huge television that he knew had cost quite a bit, since his friend had saved for months to buy the stupid thing. It saddened him to think that Gerald had worked so hard for something that meant absolutely nothing now.

Tammy stared at the impressive DVD display with her fists on her hips, as if having no idea where to start, while he wandered over to the television. There was a DVD player underneath, as well as a receiver for satellite television. He shook his head again; if only they'd known what was coming, they would have spent every penny on stocking up on food. And maybe guns and ammo.

Just to the right of the player, Nathan could see something half-hidden under it. Curious, he bent to retrieve it and had to lift the player to pull it out. It was a DVD case and Nathan laughed when he read what it was. Tammy turned to look at him, a question on her face.

He held up the DVD. "Marilyn Monroe movie," he told her. "*Gentlemen Prefer Blondes*," he read, then waved the box. "One of the songs from that movie is—"

"'Diamonds Are A Girl's Best Friend'," Tammy interrupted, laughing as she turned back toward the kitchen.

Nathan grinned at her. "Yeah, but someone took a marker and changed it to a 'Guy's' best friend."

"Well, Mr. Diamond," she said over her shoulder, "guess you have your date."

"And code," Nathan added as he followed.

He spun the dial several times, then stopped on the month, turned back to the day, then spun again for the year. He tugged on the handle, but it didn't budge. He paused for a moment, then realized Gerald would have likely used the day, month and year format.

Still nothing.

"Hmm," Nathan murmured as he thought. He startled when Tammy grabbed his hand and said, "Let's pray." He winced. *Not again.*

"Father, we need Your help again. Help my husband remember the last day he had lunch with Gerald. Show him what the combination to that lock is. Amen."

Nathan silently thanked the universe that she'd at least kept the prayer short, though he was agitated with her constant need to talk to a non-existent entity. He shook his head, then focused on the task at hand.

The combination *had* to be the date, since it was so obviously hinted at on the calendar. And Gerald had said the combination was the last time they'd had lunch.

He thought back to that day and fought to remember everything. They'd arrived at the diner within minutes of each other and didn't have to wait for a table, because Margie always saved the corner booth in the back for them every Wednesday at twelve-thirty. No matter how busy the restaurant was, no one ever complained about the two police officers receiving preferential treatment. In fact, the townsfolk seemed to expect it and even welcome it.

That was the day Nathan had seen his doctor to get his test results. His friend had been after him for weeks to see a physician for the tremors and tics, but it wasn't until his right lower leg had started to go numb that he'd finally relented. And then wished he hadn't once he'd received the diagnosis.

Some things are better off not knowing.

It was at that meal that he'd confessed to Gerald what Doctor Riggs had told him. Gerald had tears in his eyes as he'd promised he and Felicia would watch over Tammy, to help her through the grieving process and to make sure she got back on her feet. Nathan had been too numb at the time to truly appreciate what his friend was offering, though he'd nodded his thanks.

He shook those morbid thoughts away and tried to concentrate on other things. The busy diner. Dane Olsen walking in and greeting everyone in his booming voice that commanded attention. Margie spilling a glass of water on Georgie O'Sullivan, who joked he would tip her extra if she dried him off. *"Dirty old man,"* Nathan had muttered. *"Well, at least he has one clean spot now,"* Gerald had retorted.

Nathan could see the yellow plate before him with the double meat, double cheeseburger he'd ordered, the same thing he always ordered. The onion rings had been slightly overcooked that day.

Gerald had ordered the special, as always. That day it was an open meatloaf sandwich, complete with garlic mashed potatoes and brown gravy. Usually, Nathan teased Gerald about the amount of food he was able to consume without gaining weight, but he hadn't been in a joking mood that day. After admitting what the doctor had told him, he'd barely said two words.

His friend had tried to make idle conversation as he ate, while Nathan picked at his food. *"I love when they have meatloaf,"* he'd said as he chewed around a large bite. *"But my favorite is chicken fried steak. That's the best."*

Why he remembered that conversation, Nathan couldn't say. The day was mostly a blur, as were the weeks to follow, yet he somehow now remembered almost everything they'd talked about. All the inane, stupid chatter...

A thought occurred to him then and with wide eyes, he stepped to the lock again, spinning the dial while Tammy watched.

"One, twelve, nine," he said out loud as he maneuvered the lock. When it clicked, he grinned in triumph as he pulled the metal lever, opening the vault door.

"Nine?" Tammy asked as she followed him into the darkened room. Nathan felt around for a light switch, then remembered there was no electricity. Feeling foolish, he started to turn around to walk back into the kitchen to look for a flashlight or a candle, but the light suddenly came on. He looked up to see LED lights overhead, apparently battery powered, and motion activated.

He glanced at his wife. "Nine is the number on the menu for the open-faced meatloaf sandwich at the diner," he explained. He shrugged. "Don't ask me how I remember that. You know how much I hate meatloaf." Although he knew that if a slice of the once-dreaded meat mixture was put in front of him then, he'd eat it up without question or hesitation. His stomach growled at the thought of it.

Tammy grinned at him. "God revealed it to you." Nathan gave her a look that said what he thought of that, and she chuckled.

Unlike the false pantry entry, the room revealed by the vault door was a large space lined with shelves, something typically found in farmhouses, where plenty of food needed to be stored to feed the masses.

There were the usual canned goods—vegetables, meats, fruits. Convenience foods such as the canned pastas he'd loved so much as a kid. Packages of commercial freeze-dried meals were stacked there as well. Cases of bottled water filled another shelf, along with foil fruit juice packs and small cans of vegetable juice. But what caught his eye and made him want to weep was on the bottom shelf.

Two handguns and a rifle, along with boxes of ammo. And two folded gunnysacks.

Nathan was an expert marksman and had earned a certificate for qualifying at the very top of his class at the police academy. But since he'd been dismissed from the department, he'd had to turn in his weapons. At the time, knowing the reason why he'd been let go, he thought it might not have been a bad idea to keep him away from firearms. His mental state had been fragile, to say the least. He honestly couldn't say that he would have been trustworthy with a weapon in those early, bleak days after his prognosis.

But once the Neos came on the scene, he'd felt vulnerable. The rumors of the horrors committed by the Neos soldiers were terrifying, to say the least. There was no way he could have defended himself or Tammy from the group should they have targeted them as their next victims.

Walking the twenty miles from town to Gerald's house had also been an exercise in keeping calm while knowing he had no way to defend them. It had really hit home when those men on the ATVs had come up, stopping just feet from them. Hiding behind a rock with nothing more than the water bottles in his backpack to use as a weapon had not been something he'd ever wish to repeat. He was still shaking his head over the fact that the men had moved on without seeing them, especially since Nathan hadn't been able to cover their tracks well enough before he had to hide.

He wondered if the weapons had been left by Gerald, that his friend might have assumed he and Tammy would show up. It would make sense, since it was obvious the combination for the lock had been keyed for Nathan only. But he didn't want to take anything from his friend's stockpile unless he knew for sure.

That's when he saw a folded piece of paper tucked under one of the nine millimeters. He pulled it out and unfolded it.

Hey Bud—

If you're reading this, guess you figured out the combo. Sorry we're not there, but we had to bug out. Neos came by and told me I had to "report for duty." Yeah. As if. We left the next day.

Take whatever you want, but don't stay in the house. Not safe. You remember that other place I have— where we drank beer until the girls were mad. Rest there until you're ready, but Fel and I want you to join us. We're heading to Reed's. You remember where that is. Got some like-minded there. Be like a hippie commune.

Take care. Love ya bro.

Ger.

Tammy leaned over his shoulder and read the note. "Reed's?" she asked. He knew she didn't have to ask about "that other place," since she likely hadn't forgotten the night he had gone with Gerald into the storm cellar at the back of the property. Leaving the girls to watch whatever girlie movie they'd put on, the men had consumed nearly a full case of beer, laughing and making fun of their fellow officers and the citizens of the town. It hadn't been their finest moment, but it had been one of the best memories Nathan had of his friend.

Tammy and Felicia had not been happy with them. Not at all.

"Reed is Felicia's dad," he told her. "I guess they went to go stay with him."

Tammy nodded. Though she was friends with Felicia, he knew that the two weren't as close as he and Gerald had been. They'd likely never discussed

53

their families much. That sort of small talk was reserved for those few people in one's life that could be trusted with the deepest, darkest secrets, and he knew without a doubt that he was the only one in Tammy's life she trusted with hers.

He wished he didn't know those dark secrets of hers, because every time he thought about it, he wanted to dig her dad up and make sure he was truly dead.

"Where is that?" she asked as she stared at the weapons. Tammy hated firearms of any type, so Nathan knew he'd be the one packing for the next leg of their journey.

And it was a whopper of a journey.

He sighed and ran a weary hand over his face, fisting it when he noticed the tremor was still present. Soon, he wouldn't be able to hide his condition from her.

Nathan glanced down at the tired-looking woman by his side. He figured they'd fill the sacks with as much food as they could carry, then head to the storm cellar and sleep for a few days. Or more.

He sighed deeply, his shoulders lifting in the process. "Florida Keys."

THE STORM cellar was smaller than Nathan remembered, but it was better than staying in the huge farmhouse, wondering if the Neos were going to come knocking. He'd gladly breathe in the dank, musty air and deal with bumping into Tammy every five minutes on the twin-sized bed not designed for two adults, if it meant they could get some sleep without worrying what might be coming their way.

He had no idea how long they'd been in the cellar, though he guesstimated at least two days, since he'd opened the cellar door a few times to check the area. Once it had been in the heat of the day; another, in the pitch black of night. Time passed in an unfathomable way when you didn't have windows or a clock.

The Bonavitas had stocked the cellar with all the essentials, though when they'd been in the house pantry, Tammy had filled the gunnysacks with everything she could fit, which was most of it. The metal shelf along the wall was packed from top to bottom. Nathan had laughed when he saw how much she was packing.

"We're not gonna be here that long," he told her. "Couple of days, maybe three, tops."

She'd shrugged as she pulled a box of the juices from one of the bags and shoved it onto one of the shelves. "You never know. It doesn't hurt to be prepared."

That comment had given him pause. There was no way to *be* prepared, since they had no way of knowing what was coming their way.

They'd just finished eating yet again and he stood to collect their trash. They were going to have to take the garbage bag out soon before it started to stink, though he had no idea what to do with it. Gerald had a burn barrel for trash, but Nathan didn't want to start a fire. That was a sure way to show the enemy their location.

As he smashed the empty food containers down, he thought about how they'd eaten more in the past few days than they had in months. It was rather nice not to have to ration, since they'd been eating all the canned foods and saving the lighter freeze-dried meals for traveling.

He wasn't looking forward to that. Not at all.

But Nathan figured there wasn't much choice. When they'd decided to leave their hometown before the Neos locked the place down insuring that they *couldn't* leave, he didn't have a plan past getting to Gerald's. His friend's little farm had meant safety and security, somewhere far away from those who were causing far more harm than good.

If there was some sort of community, like the one Gerald had mentioned, that would welcome them in and would be a place where Tammy could live once he was gone, then he was willing to go the distance. And what a distance it was.

He'd found a map Gerald had left for them in the cellar that had a very faint line drawn on it indicating the path that should be taken to get to their destination. If you didn't know the general direction you were to take, you never would have noticed the line. It stretched all the way from the southeast border of Indiana and Kentucky to a beach near Tallahassee. It was a very long line.

When Nathan had been a senior in high school, he and some friends had decided to head to Florida for Spring break. That trip had taken them over fifteen hours of driving to get to Daytona Beach.

It was going to take them literal months to walk to Florida.

But it couldn't be helped. It wasn't like they could live in Gerald's storm cellar for the rest of their lives. It was probably just a matter of time before the Neos came looking for the man who was likely on a deserter list. Nathan wondered if the men on the ATVs had actually been after Gerald and Felicia. That made more sense, since he and Tammy were non-entities as far as the Neos were concerned.

At least for now.

"Hey, I want to take a shower or a bath," Tammy said, startling him out of his thoughts as he tied up the garbage bag. Nathan sighed at the thought of all the work involved to make that happen, but he couldn't blame her. He felt gritty and nasty himself.

"Okay." He hefted the bag and carried it to the small cellar door. Gerald told him the real estate agent said the previous owners had dug the storm cellar in the woods during the Cold War crisis, thinking that the Russians were going to invade the U.S. and wanted somewhere they could hide. It was completely hidden from the rest of the property, and unless you knew where to look, you'd never see the entrance. Nathan had barely managed to find it when he and Tammy had ventured into the woods the first morning.

Nathan cracked the door open and noted the long shadows, indicating it was nearing dusk. Though the cellar was hidden from the house, he still remained very cautious as he glanced around, making sure the woods were clear, listening for any engine noise.

It was quiet. Maybe too quiet.

Tammy said she wondered where all the animals had gone. She'd made the comment that for the past few weeks she hadn't seen even one bird. Truthfully, Nathan hadn't noticed. He'd been too busy avoiding the two-legged variety of animal, which had become mostly crazed, wild beasts.

He would never understand how humans could turn on each other in a crisis. Yet, he'd seen it over and over since the economy crashed. At first, neighbors would help neighbors, sharing food and supplies. But when people started realizing the economy wasn't going to "bounce back" like the president kept assuring everyone it would, well... society took a hard right turn.

And then the president and his entire cabinet disappeared over night. Cue the appearance of the Neo Geo Task Force.

He glanced over his shoulder, smiling slightly when he saw Tammy cleaning the cellar once again. They hadn't had much to do, other than eat and sleep, and she seemed happy to occupy herself with tidying the place up. He supposed it was a good thing, since one of her cleaning sprees had turned up a small crossbow, which Tammy had decided she would carry instead of a firearm. It made Nathan feel a bit better, knowing that his wife had some way of protecting herself if something happened to him.

When something happens...

He told himself those thoughts were better left in the back of his mind, because he had more important things to worry about for the time being. Like figuring out how they were going to get enough water to bathe.

"It's almost dark," he told Tammy as he closed the cellar door. "A few more minutes and we'll head out." He sighed as he sat on the bed. "Just not sure how we're gonna pull off a shower though."

"A bath is fine," she said as she bent to dust off a shelf that had no dust, thanks to her earlier cleaning.

"Same problem," Nathan said with a grimace that she didn't see.

She straightened and turned toward him. "What do you mean?"

He shrugged. "No electricity, so no water. The

pump won't run without power."

Tammy's mouth dropped open. "Oh," she said, then smiled, an embarrassed look on her face as she waved her fingers.

"City girl here. I'm used to having water no matter what. I figured we'd have to take cold showers, but I never thought about not having water at all," she said with a slight whine to her voice. Nathan didn't blame her; he'd been looking forward to a shower too.

"You would think the Bonavitas would have had solar installed," she added.

He nodded. "Yeah..." He tilted his head, then shook it. "They might have. We didn't actually try anything to see if there was power. I just assumed there wasn't. Especially with that old-fashioned vault lock."

Tammy nodded. "Yeah, me too."

He stood. "Well, c'mon, let's find out."

It wasn't completely dark like Nathan would have preferred, but dusk had fallen to the point where there were no more shadows. They walked to the edge of the forest clearing and he held out his arm to stop Tammy from proceeding. She huffed. He knew that she thought he was paranoid and overly cautious, but he didn't care. He was going to do everything he could to make sure they weren't spotted by the Neos.

They wouldn't be shuttled off to the dissident camps, not if he could help it.

Once he was certain there were no vehicles or people in the area, they stepped out of the dark of the forest and trotted to the back of the house. Nathan had locked the place up when they'd gone to the cellar, but he'd left one of the back windows unlatched. It slid up without any noise and he poked his head inside, listening.

"Wait here," he murmured to Tammy as he pulled himself up onto the windowsill. "I'll open the back door."

Once they were inside, he pulled the chain on a small table lamp and jumped when it turned on. Tammy laughed.

"Well, I guess that means there's electricity. And water!"

Nathan grinned, glad that his wife was so happy. He quickly turned the lamp off, then they made their way upstairs and into the master bedroom.

"Let me find something to put over the bathroom window," he told her as he started opening the drawers of a chest. He was surprised to see that Gerald had left most of his clothes behind, but then he figured that they would be traveling light too, especially since it was such a far way to go. He wondered how far his friends had gotten by now.

Tammy crossed her arms over her chest and glared at him, though she didn't comment. Nathan ignored her as he pulled out a black sweatshirt, then went back downstairs to find something to secure it to the window. He went to the toolbox he'd seen earlier in the mudroom at the back of the house and dug through it, finding a hammer and some nails.

The bedroom was almost completely dark when he walked back in, but he could see Tammy's outline as she sat on the bed.

"Just take a second," he told her as he walked into the bathroom, cursing when he banged his shin on the toilet. He quickly tacked the sweatshirt over the small window, then called for Tammy to come into the room.

Once she did as he asked, he closed the door behind them and then rolled one of the towels hanging on the rack into a tube and shoved it into the crack under the door. When that was done, he turned on the light.

Tammy remained quiet while she turned the water on, though she let out a squeal of delight after a moment. "It's hot!" she laughed, then adjusted the temperature and started to strip.

"I hope Felicia left some clothes," she said as she pulled her filthy t-shirt over her head. "Or I guess I could just wash these."

Nathan shook his head. "I don't want to stay in the house any longer than we have to. But Gerald's dresser was full, so I'm sure Felicia's is too." He started to strip, as well, anxious to get the filth off his body. And the stench.

Once they were clean and dried, they searched through their friends' clothes. "Find something more earth tone," he told Tammy.

"It's kind of hard to tell what color anything is without the light on," she said drolly.

Nathan glanced at the bedroom window, though he couldn't see it in the dark. He cautiously made his way toward it, slowly navigating the unfamiliar room. His shin still throbbed where he'd hit it earlier and he didn't want a repeat.

The window had a heavy curtain, but it also had a blackout shade. He should have known that it would, since Felicia worked the nightshift as a nurse and would sleep during the day. Once the shade was secured and the curtains pulled closed, he turned on a bedside lamp.

Tammy went into the Bonavita's closet and dug

around in there while Nathan opened the nightstand drawers, hoping to find more ammo. He didn't, but he did find a small survival-type tool that he tucked into the shorts he wore. They were almost identical to his own that were now on the floor of the bathroom, though Gerald was a little larger around the midsection and he'd had to add a belt to keep them from sliding off his hips. Tammy had been several sizes larger than Felicia, which would have been an issue for her taking the woman's clothes, but Nathan knew his wife was probably the same size now, if not smaller.

He rubbed at the ache in his chest when he thought about how little they'd been able to eat the past few months.

Though Tammy would roll her eyes and call him a Neanderthal if he mentioned it, it bothered him that he hadn't been able to provide for her. If only he'd known what was coming, if he'd had some sort of warning, he would have stockpiled food and the things they needed to live. But, like everyone else, he'd been blindsided.

But not Gerald and Felicia...

His friends had certainly planned ahead. Food, water, guns and ammo. That vault door had to be installed long before the economic collapse. Nathan had never known his friends were "preppers," but then he realized that he would have teased Gerald mercilessly if he had known. And that was probably why the man had kept it to himself.

Despite knowing that Nathan would have given him a hard time, Gerald had still made sure that he took care of himself and Felicia, plus provided for them as well. It was a very unselfish gesture, but Nathan knew that was just how Gerald and his wife were. Good people.

He was brought out of his thoughts by another squeal from Tammy. He laughed quietly; his wife was easily excited at times.

"What'd you find?" he called out, though he still kept his voice down. Just in case.

Tammy walked out of the closet, some clothes draped over her arm. But that wasn't what had excited her. Instead, she was staring down at the object in her hands, a very happy grin on her face. When Nathan stepped closer to see what she held, he had to fight back a groan. He was afraid his life just got a whole lot worse.

A Bible. Ugh.

Chapter 4

NATE, STOP." Tammy hated to ask again, but she just couldn't walk another step without a break. It seemed like they'd walked hours since the last time they stopped to rest, but she knew it was probably less than one.

She hated being a bother, especially when Nate sighed loudly, though thankfully he didn't comment. This time, anyway. She knew he was getting more and more frustrated each day.

It had been four days since they'd left the safety and relative comfort of the cellar in the woods. Though it had been cramped and stuffy, Tammy had appreciated not feeling like she had to look over her shoulder every few moments. After the ordeal in the woods with the riders, she'd been feeling a bit more paranoid. Not on the scale that her husband was, but still...

And she knew that it was wrong to feel that way, because the Lord had brought them through that, and He'd bring them through whatever came their way next.

They made their way off the road, where they found an area that suited Nate's need to hide whenever they rested. Tammy knew that the very long trip to Florida was going to test both their patience and their marriage. She was getting tired of his overbearing protectiveness, and she knew he was weary of her need for constant rest and potty breaks. *Or rock breaks,* she thought to herself.

She sighed as she tugged off the heavy backpack. Besides her aching feet and legs, her shoulders and neck were throbbing and burning. They'd packed as much food and supplies as they could carry out of necessity, but the burden was becoming a bit much for her. She just wasn't built for being a pack mule.

Tammy kept her groans and moans to herself, though. She knew that Nate's pack was far heavier than her own, since he insisted on carrying most of the bottles of water, while she had the much lighter freeze-dried food packs and a change of clothes for the both of them.

And her precious "stolen" Bible.

She wished she could read it when they stopped for a rest, but even with the moonlight they now had to guide their steps, it was simply too dark. But once they stopped for the day, she made sure to read at least several chapters in both the Old and New Testaments.

It was a strange thing—before she'd backslidden, she'd always been a reader of the Word. But now that she'd recommitted herself to the Lord and started trusting Him more and more, the Scripture seemed to be leaping off the pages at her. It was as the pastors always said—it truly was "the living Word."

Nate pulled his pack off and shrugged his shoulders, as if trying to get some blood back into them. Even in the pale moonlight, Tammy could see the deep grooves the straps left in his muscles. Though she was bone-tired and just wanted to fall flat on her back and take a little nap, she pushed up and moved toward him, sitting behind him. He looked at her over his shoulder, his eyebrow raised in question.

She didn't say anything as she reached out and started to rub his shoulders. Nate tensed at first as she pushed into the tight muscles, but as she worked at the knots, he relaxed and released a low moan. She rubbed until her hands cramped, then patted him on the back.

"Thank you," he muttered, then reached down and snagged her by the ankle. She started to ask him what he was doing, but he pulled her sneaker off and started rubbing her foot. Like her husband, she tensed at first as the pain was almost too much to bear, but in just a few moments, she, too, was moaning in relief.

Once he was done with her other foot, she put her shoes back on and then pulled out a bottle of water for them to share. They were trying to be very conservative and would refill the bottles whenever they found a good water source, but those were few and far between. Other than a few flowing streams and one abandoned farmhouse with an old-fashioned hand pump, they hadn't had much luck.

She handed Nate a piece of turkey jerky and they ate their snack in silence. There were a million things she wanted to say, and to ask, but there were times when it was just easier not to talk at all. And sometimes it was safer.

That was a hard lesson she'd learned early on from her father, who held to the belief not only that "children should be seen and not heard," but that "females had nothing to say that anyone wanted to hear." Her mother had been as beaten down as she had been, though Tammy held her at fault for not getting them out of a bad situation.

She winced at her thoughts. *Father, I need Your help to forgive my mom and dad. Even though my dad is dead, I know that I need to let go of all that resentment. And forgive me for not talking to my mom all these years, especially now that we're going through such hard times...*

Her mind wandered away from her prayer and she started thinking about all the evil that had seemed to take over the world overnight. Of course, she knew that the evil had always been there, but it was as if a cork had been popped off the bottle, letting it just explode all over the place.

It was a terrifying time to be on earth, she thought. She knew it was only going to get worse. The Bible study her youth pastor had led when she'd been a young teen had scared Tammy a lot. The Book of Revelation was very clear about how awful it would be. But Pastor Gene had assured them that believers didn't need to worry about suffering through the Tribulation, that they wouldn't be on earth during that time.

Tammy still wondered about that, wondered if the Rapture as she'd been taught would happen, and hopefully, soon. But she still questioned everything. She'd always heard that the church couldn't be on earth with the antichrist, but since the Neos had arrived on the scene, and there was no doubt they were working for Satan himself, she doubted believers were going to be "taken up" beforehand. It seemed the antichrist had already arrived.

It was all pretty confusing.

One thing was certain, though—she didn't want to be around for the end times. One way or another, she hoped she was taken off the earth by then. She glanced at Nate, who was trying to read the map Gerald had left for them.

Father, help me get through to my husband. Give me the right words to reach him. Don't let him die without accepting You as his Savior.

"Ready?" Nate asked as he pushed himself up,

bringing her out of her thoughts. She nodded reluctantly, though she wanted to cry and beg him for more time to rest. But she knew he would urge her on, insisting that they had to "get going."

She really had no idea why he was pushing them so hard. From watching the mile markers on the two-lane highway they were traveling down, she knew they were walking at least twenty-five miles a night, sometimes over thirty. There were times when she argued against going any farther, telling Nate he could just leave her behind, that she'd had enough and didn't care if they made it to Florida or not.

But most times she just tried her best to keep pace with him.

He seemed almost desperate to get to their destination. And she was starting to suspect it had something to do with the tremor in his hand, the tic in his cheek and the fact that he was dragging his foot more and more.

She let herself go down a road of worry for a bit, but then stopped herself and said a quick prayer, asking the Lord to forgive her once again for not trusting Him. But there was no reason why she shouldn't at least know what she was facing.

"Nate..." she started but paused. Her husband was even tighter-lipped than she was at times. He glanced at her and she waved her hand, motioning toward his body. "What's going on with you?"

In the dim light, she could see him frown. "What do you mean?"

Tammy sighed softly. "With your... health." He started to immediately argue, but she put her hand up.

"I know there's something wrong. Something you're not telling me." Tammy made sure her tone was as stern as she could make it. "I've seen your hand shaking. The tic in your face. And sometimes you drag your foot." She stopped walking and turned to him. He seemed reluctant to stop, but he did and looked at her, a stubborn set to his face.

She crossed her arms. "I'm not moving another inch until you tell me what's going on," she stressed. "For Pete's sake, we've been married for nearly ten years, and you *still* don't trust me?" She hated the way her voice choked on that, but her emotions were suddenly riding high. She'd held her tongue for weeks now, but no more. She had a right to know what was going on.

"It's not that," he said as he ran that shaking hand over the back of his neck. He paused, then put his hand out and stared at it like it was offensive. He fisted his fingers, then dropped his arm and sighed as he tilted his head back and looked heavenward. Tammy wished that he was doing so in prayer, but she knew he was just thinking about what to tell her. Or rather, *how* to tell her.

She started worrying again and wondered if she really wanted to hear what he had to say.

Another sigh lifted her husband's shoulders, and then he surprised her by reaching out to pull her into his chest. She winced at the acrid smell of his sweat but knew that she didn't smell any better.

"I've got... a condition," he said, hedging. "It's what's causing the, uh, tremors."

She knew there was a lot he wasn't telling her, and she poked him in the ribs on both sides. "Tell me," she encouraged.

Another sigh. "It's..." He paused, then cleared his throat. "It's Creutzfeldt-Jakob disease."

Tammy frowned; she never heard of it before. "What is—"

"It's... a dementia type disease. Kinda like Alzheimer's, but... worse. Much worse."

She sucked in a breath. She knew what the final prognosis was for Alzheimer's patients and if this was worse... "Is it—"

"Fatal? Yeah," he said blandly, like he just told her that his hairline was receding. Tammy felt like the world was crashing down around her. Needing to see his face, she pushed out of his arms, though he kept his hands on her biceps. She put her hands on his chest.

"How long?" she whispered, afraid to know the answer. While they might have drifted apart emotionally, Nate had been her rock for so long she couldn't imagine life without him. And he was young, far too young to have a disease like that. She wanted to yell at God that it wasn't fair.

He shrugged. "Doctor said maybe a year. Possibly less. By the time I went to see him, he said that I was already showing some end stage symptoms," Nathan said blandly, like he was giving her a grocery list. "There's no way to tell how fast it'll progress."

Feeling like her world was reeling, Tammy struggled to take a deep enough breath to fill her lungs. She could feel the beginning of a panic attack coming on, and fought against it, trying to remember all the things her therapist had told her—breathe deeply, count to ten, count backwards from ten, focus on slowing her heartbeat.

She closed her eyes as she struggled to calm herself, though her mind immediately went to contemplating life without Nate. It was truly impossible. Once he was gone... she shook her thoughts away from the direction they were heading. She just knew that she'd be alone in the world. No more friends, no more family. No more husband.

Opening her eyes once again, Tammy shook her head—not in denial, but in disbelief. Her eyes filled and she stared at her husband numbly as he moved his hand from her arm and wiped at the wet streams flowing down her cheeks.

"It'll be all right," he said, but she could hear the doubt in his voice. "Gerald and Felicia said you were welcome to stay with them—"

"Wait, you mean Gerald knows?" she said, the last word coming out more like a shriek. Her tears of anguish turned to anger. Nate winced and put his finger to her lips.

"Don't yell," he warned, always vigilantly aware of their surroundings. But Tammy was tired of caring about the world, about the Neos, about those who might want to cause them harm. In that moment, she was ready to pick a fight with someone.

"I'll yell if I want to," she growled at him. "I can't believe you'd tell Gerald, but not your own wife!" The idea of it made her want to punch him, hard. Either that or burst into tears and run as far away as her aching feet would allow. Which would probably only be a few dozen yards.

Nate sighed again as he released her and stepped back, as if he were afraid of her. *Good,* she thought. *You should be afraid of me, buddy.*

He held his hands up. "I know, I know. It's just

72

that I met Gerald for lunch right after I came from the doctor's, after I got the test results. He knew just by looking at me that it wasn't good."

"And yet he knew that you'd gone to the doctor, while that was something else you kept from *your wife*! Ugh!" She turned and stomped off, though she continued down the road in the direction they'd been heading. She heard Nate's footsteps hurrying to catch up, but she ignored him.

"I didn't want to worry you for no reason," he said as he trotted up. "I'd been feeling off—"

"Something else you never told me," she hissed, then continued ignoring him.

He sighed. "Again, didn't want to worry you. I was getting these tremors and Gerald insisted I go see the doc."

Tammy wanted to lash out at him again, but she knew it was out of hurt more than anger. Though if she were honest with herself, she was more angry at herself for not noticing that her husband was having issues. It made her realize that she'd been too wrapped up in her own life, with her own job and friends, to pay much attention to the man she'd pledged her earthly life to.

She sighed, a defeated sound, as she forced herself to let go of her hurt. Now wasn't the time to have any problems between them. They needed to be on the same team. She reached out and grabbed both his hands.

"I'm sorry for getting upset. I know you don't like it when I worry. But I'm trying hard not to do that anymore, and just put everything in God's capable hands." She smiled at him, though his expression turned sour at her words.

"We can't go on like that anymore, honey," she continued. "We need to communicate, to let each other know what's going on. We've been really bad about that the past few years." She winced when she realized just how true that was; when they were first married, they shared their wishes, their dreams, even their fears. But they seemed to have drifted apart with each anniversary, to the point that they confided in friends first.

Nate nodded. "Yeah," he agreed, a tired, defeated sound. Tammy squeezed his hands and then they turned and started walking again. She kept a hold on his hand.

"The doctor gave you a year," she said, surprised her voice was so steady.

"Maybe less, maybe more," he said with another shrug.

She was quiet for a moment. "Well, honestly, I'm pretty sure there isn't that much time left for any of us."

Out of the corner of her eye, she saw him glance at her. "What do you mean?"

Tammy said a quick prayer, asking for the right words, those that wouldn't offend him or upset him, or make him close off to the Holy Spirit's work.

"I know you hate hearing it, but the Bible talks about this," she said with a wave. "The end times. I'm pretty sure we're there now. Or at least, really, really close."

He made a scoffing sound. "And you really believe that?"

"Yep," Tammy said with certainty. "I do. I'm pretty sure we're gonna see a lot of stuff from Bible prophesy come true, come to pass, here real soon."

Nate made another sound. "Like what?" She knew he didn't do it intentionally, but his tone was mocking. She squeezed his hand slightly.

"New one world government, for one." She shrugged. "Pretty sure the Neos are it. I mean, even their name—Neo Geo Task Force—screams that. And one world currency. With the economic crash that affected every single country that we know of, that's probably already in the works." She didn't mention the one world religion; Nate was antagonistic as it was.

That time, he made a thoughtful sound. "Think you'd have to show me where it says that before I'll believe it."

Tammy's heart beat a bit faster at his words. She'd tried reading Scripture to him before, once she'd gotten Felicia's Bible, but he'd always put a stop to it. Now he was actually asking to hear it? She knew that was from the Lord.

"When we stop for the day, I'll show you," she promised. At her words, he glanced at the sky and her eyes followed, surprised to see the faint glow of the dawn already on the horizon. Tammy wanted to cry in relief.

They'd taken to camping outside most of the time. Nate had mentioned being glad that it was still late summer; otherwise, they'd be struggling to survive a Midwest winter. Though she really wished they'd had shelter every day—and especially one with indoor plumbing—Tammy had started to enjoy sleeping in the shade of a tree.

"We better stop soon," Nate murmured as he glanced around. The moon was nearly full, something she'd been thankful for as they'd walked along unfamiliar roads. She didn't think she'd even driven down the road they were on in the past.

Nate was keeping them on a mostly southern path, though she knew they were also heading slightly eastward. He'd mentioned wanting to get to the southern states as soon as possible. "The farther south we are then, the less chance of it getting cold," he'd said. It made sense to her, especially since they only had warm weather clothing.

He pointed to the west of the road. "Over there," he said. Tammy squinted to see where he was indicating and could see what looked like a very long building. She stared harder and realized it was an abandoned train. She thought it was strange that it would have been left out in the middle of nowhere like that, but she wasn't going to look a gift-shelter in the window.

They made their way across the field toward the tracks, stepping carefully in case of snakes. But, again, Tammy figured they wouldn't see any; the animals seemed to have better sense than the humans and had gotten out while they could. Where they could have gone was anyone's guess.

She knew the drill as they approached the train car—no talking, watch your step so you didn't make any noise, let Nate go first to check things out. Her overprotective husband might be aggravating, but she certainly couldn't fault him for sticking to his vigilance. She might have thought it was overblown, but he was consistent.

As they drew closer, the dawn's glow lit up the side of the train, revealing a rainbow of colors that had been painted along the bottom half. Graffiti covered the train as far as she could see and she wondered if the crude artwork had been completed before the crash, or if some kids with nothing better to do had decided to showcase their talent after the fact. Probably before, since spray paint was most certainly a luxury item few could afford these days.

The first set of the train's doors were closed, and Nate kept walking. Tammy was surprised to see all the windows were intact; she figured the graffiti artists would have had a field day with further vandalizing. It wasn't like anyone was going to stop them.

Of course, most people were occupied with trying to survive, not destroy property.

She shook her head slightly. That wasn't entirely true. Before they'd left their hometown, Tammy had witnessed several acts of senseless destruction. People throwing rocks and bricks through windows, slashing tires, and even lighting fires in their neighbor's yards. And then there was the burning of the church...

Her eyes filled as she thought about that night. That little church had meant so much to her—both good and bad. It was a place for comfort, where her Sunday School teachers would kindly guide her to learn about Jesus and led her to know more about the faith they clung to.

It was also a place where Tammy learned how to put on a "church face." Showing what she truly felt would be met with punishment more severe than she cared to think about.

Shaking those thoughts away, she silently followed her husband to a door near the middle of the train. It was light enough outside to see that it was slightly ajar. She waited while Nate crept up to it, then put his ear to the opening. It was a long while before he seemed to be satisfied that it was safe, though he turned to her and put his finger to his lips. She rolled her eyes; she knew by now that he didn't want her to make a sound whenever they approached a new place.

Prying the doors open—which were surprisingly free of squeaks or squeals—Nate pulled a handgun from his pocket as he walked up the steps, into the train car. Tammy glanced around the area, watching for any movement. Nate had warned her to always be on the lookout for an ambush, for someone watching and waiting for them to let their guard down before attacking. It gave her goosebumps to think about being vulnerable out in the open, and she pulled the crossbow that hung by a strap from her shoulder around to her front, then nocked an arrow.

She kept her back to the train as she looked around, but then thought about someone hiding under the train, which caused her to hop away and turn. There was no movement from under the train, either, but she kept a few yards away and turned in a slow circle.

"Psst!" She glanced up to see Nate standing in the doorway, motioning to her. He smiled and nodded approvingly when he saw that she had her weapon at the ready. She didn't share the information that the bow wasn't cocked; truthfully, Tammy knew she wasn't strong enough to pull the mechanism back, though she'd never told Nate. She wanted to give the illusion that she was capable of protecting herself, which was more lie than anything else. She had absolutely no training whatsoever in defense.

She moved toward the train and climbed the steps, looking around as she did. The train looked completely deserted, but it was hard to tell for sure. She figured Nate had already checked the car out, though, so she moved away from the door, toward the back of the car. Dropping her backpack and crossbow onto a seat, she plopped down next to them and sighed in relief. It was good to sit.

It was a little while later when she leaned over and pulled her Bible out. Nate had taken the seats across the aisle from her and had his eyes closed, but Tammy knew he probably wasn't asleep. The man would stay alert and vigilant for several hours, at least until he was sure no one was going to crawl out from under a seat or something and ambush them.

Praying first that the Lord would lead her to find the right passages, Tammy opened her Bible and turned to the Book of Revelation. She had to search for a moment but came to the exact passage she'd had in mind. She silently thanked the Lord, then began to read quietly out loud.

"From the Book of Revelation: 'And the dragon stood on the sand of the seashore. Then I saw a beast coming up out of the sea, having ten horns and seven heads, and on his horns were ten diadems, and on his heads were blasphemous names. And the beast which I saw was like a leopard, and his feet were like those of a bear, and his mouth like the mouth of a lion. And the dragon gave him his power and his throne and great authority. I saw one of his heads as if it had been slain, and his fatal wound was healed. And the whole earth was amazed and followed after the beast; they worshiped the dragon because he gave his authority to the beast; and they worshiped the beast, saying, "Who is like the beast, and who is able to wage war with him?"'"

She then felt led to turn to Daniel and rifled through the pages, surprised, yet not too much so, when she found exactly what she needed. "In the Book of Daniel, chapter seven: 'I approached one of those who were standing by'—these were angels," she explained, "—and began asking him the exact meaning of all this. So he told me and made known to me the interpretation of these things: "These great beasts, which are four in number, are four kings who will arise from the earth. But the saints of the Highest One will receive the kingdom and possess the kingdom forever, for all ages to come." Then I desired to know the exact meaning of the fourth beast, which was different from all the others, exceedingly dreadful, with its teeth of iron and its claws of bronze, and which devoured, crushed and trampled down the remainder with its feet, and the meaning of the ten horns that were on its head and the other horn which came up, and before which three of them fell, namely, that horn which had eyes and a mouth uttering great boasts and which was larger in appearance than its associates. I kept looking, and that horn was waging war with the saints and overpowering them until the Ancient of Days came and judgment was passed in favor of the saints of the Highest One, and the time arrived when the saints took possession of the kingdom.

"'Thus he said: "The fourth beast will be a fourth kingdom on the earth, which will be different from all the other kingdoms and will devour the whole earth and tread it down and crush it. As for the ten horns, out of this kingdom ten kings will arise; and another will arise after them, and he will be different from the previous ones and will subdue three kings."'"

She turned back a few chapters, surprised she knew where to look, but knowing God was leading her.

"And in Daniel, chapter two, we have the description of the fourth beast: 'In that you saw the feet and toes, partly of potter's clay and partly of iron, it will be a divided kingdom; but it will have in it the toughness of iron, inasmuch as you saw the iron mixed with common clay. As the toes of the feet were partly of iron and partly of pottery, so some of the kingdom will be strong and part of it will be brittle.'"

She closed her Bible and looked at her husband. He still had his eyes closed, but she could tell he wasn't asleep. He'd been listening, though it seemed he wasn't going to acknowledge what she'd said.

"The coming troubles—one world government and currency and all—were all foretold thousands of years ago. And I totally believe that we're at the edge of that right now. We're moving headlong into the end of the world. Looks like we're gonna have a front-row seat."

Still no acknowledgment. Tammy sighed. "Honey, I know you don't want to hear any 'religious' stuff'," she said softly, "but if we're coming to the end of time, don't you think now's a good time to get right with God?"

Silence. Another sigh left her, this one louder than before. Setting her Bible next to her backpack, she turned and lifted the arm rests of the seats across her row, then laid back so that she was lying across the three seats. She wiggled to get comfortable and in moments, started drifting off. It was in that half-awake, half-asleep state that she heard her Bible hit the floor.

And she heard Nate pick it up.

AS HE LISTENED to Tammy read, Nathan was certain his wife was pulling rabbits out of the hat with the "end of the world" nonsense. The first Scripture she'd read didn't say anything about "one world government" or anything of the such. It might have hinted at it, but it wasn't specific. Plus, being from the New Testament, he sure wasn't going to put any stock in it. His father had always said the "false testament" of the Christians was heresy, written by men to discount Judaism.

He wasn't sure of that, but still, it was something he'd keep at arm's length until he learned otherwise.

But when Tammy had started reading from the Book of Daniel—a book he was well familiar with from his days in synagogue—well, he'd been a bit shocked. Both Scriptures seemed to line up with one another.

Of course, he told himself that the writer of that "revelation" book could have gotten his information from Daniel and used it to create a fantasy world to scare Christians into following Jesus.

He snorted to himself; he couldn't believe that Christians actually believed that Jesus—supposedly the lowly son of a carpenter—could be the actual Messiah the Jews had coveted for millennia. The Messiah was supposed to be a warrior, a conqueror of nations, a true world leader... not some stable-born no name from the tribe of Judah, of all things.

Pretending to be asleep while his wife read, he listened with half an ear, and had barely managed to keep the sigh of relief to himself when she stopped. He cracked an eye and watched her get settled in for some sleep, then started to do so himself when he heard a noise. He turned to see her Bible on the floor next to her head. Tammy didn't even flinch, already out.

Nathan stared at the offensive book for a long while, but then curiosity got the better of him. He leaned over and picked it up, careful to be quiet as he did so. The last thing he wanted was to get busted reading from something he'd discounted for so long.

Opening the book to the table of contents, he frowned when he saw the Torah—the books of Moses. It was a strange thing for Christians to include in their Bible, he thought. Equally strange was the fact that the five books of Moses were first, a place of honor.

Skipping what the Christians labeled "Old Testament," he turned to the last book, the one Tammy had read from. The first few chapters he glossed over, not finding anything too interesting. But he stopped at the sixth.

The first paragraph talked of "the Lamb"—who Nathan assumed meant Jesus—breaking seven seals. The first seal spoke of a rider, who he assumed was an angel, on a white horse, going out to conquer. The second seal was of war; the third spoke of what he assumed was the rising cost of food, since the paragraph was labeled "Famine."

Nathan frowned; if the "prophesy" was true—and he was very strongly reserving judgment on that—then it sounded like what they were going through right now. *Conqueror...* the Neo Geo Task Force.

War... while they hadn't had access to any type of newscast in months to know if war had broken out across the globe, just watching the vicious way people were treating one another now was enough to verify that. He supposed it didn't have to mean actual wars between countries, but rather, mankind warring amongst itself.

Famine... considering there was little value to money, a loaf of bread was somewhere in the region of fifty or more dollars. He and Tammy had certainly been feeling the effects of "famine."

A doubt started to form in his mind... doubting all he'd been taught about how "wrong" Christians were.

Dismissing that thought, he darted a glance at Tammy to make sure she was still asleep. He laughed to himself when he realized he'd rather she wake up and catch him looking at a pornographic magazine than reading her Bible.

The title of the next section was "Death." Nathan's frown turned to a scowl as he read to himself.

When the Lamb broke the fourth seal, I heard the voice of the fourth living creature saying, "Come." I looked, and behold, an ashen horse; and he who sat on it had the name Death; and Hades was following with him. Authority was given to them over a fourth of the earth, to kill with sword and with famine and with pestilence and by the wild beasts of the earth.

That was enough to cause him to close the book. He leaned over and placed it on the floor in the spot he'd picked it up from, then leaned back and thought about what he'd read. If it was all true—which he seriously doubted—then he really, *really* hated to know what was going to happen next.

Chapter 5

THE TRAIN CAR was a pretty comfortable place, Tammy had to admit, though it was hot. She'd opened several windows on both sides, but there wasn't even a cross breeze to cool things down and she hated the feeling of sweat trickling down her back.

The sun was still fairly high in the sky, but Nate hadn't stirred. Tammy watched her husband twitching in his sleep and wondered if it was due to a dream, or if it was due to his condition.

Over the past few days, he'd gotten worse, his hand tremor more pronounced, and his cheek jumped so violently at times it forced his eye to squint. His leg, too, had gotten worse, to the point it was him who was slowing them down, rather than her. Tammy didn't mind, though, because it was better than the break-neck pace he'd forced them to keep up with so far.

She sighed as she thought about Nate deteriorating. He hadn't shared all the details of his prognosis and she knew it was because he didn't want to worry her. She snorted to herself; as if his *dying* and leaving her behind wasn't enough of a worry. Truthfully, though, she really wasn't worried. At first, yes. But she felt like the Lord had been impressing on her that there wasn't any reason to be concerned. Time was short... for everyone.

A part of her—a really selfish part—wished that her husband wouldn't leave her behind to deal with whatever was coming on her own. The thought made her cringe at its pure selfishness but knowing that things were going to get so much worse—as in literally earth-shaking worse—made her want to have her partner at her side. But Nate would be so much better off not having to go through any of it.

Jesus, if You're coming back before the end, then I hope it's soon.

"Of course He's coming back before the end. He said He would."

Tammy startled as her eyes popped open at the voice that most certainly wasn't the Lord's—it wasn't a male voice, for one thing; for another, it was external. And just a few feet away.

A woman—no, a girl, really—was sitting in the row in front of her, arm over the back of the seat and grinning. She had to be sitting on her knees to be able to see over the tall seat, because just by her features, Tammy could tell she was a small female, even smaller than she was herself.

Tammy blinked several times, because there was no way anyone could have gotten on the train car without them hearing, especially Nate, who was always super vigilant and a very light sleeper. She glanced over at him and was shocked to see that he was still sound asleep.

The girl/woman had to have been in the car and somehow slipped their notice. She didn't know how, since she knew Nate had checked every corner. But there was just no other explanation.

But she just answered my silent prayer...

Tammy's eyes widened further, and the girl laughed, her blonde curls bobbing. "You should see yourself. You look like one of those Tarsier monkeys with the bug-eyes." She laughed louder and slapped the top of the seat. Tammy looked over at her husband once again, but he was inexplicably still asleep.

"Oh, never mind about Nathan," the girl said with a dismissive wave. "He'll stay asleep so you and I can talk."

Tammy's mouth then took its turn in showing shock as it flopped open and closed. The girl laughed even harder. "Now you look like a walleyed bass that's been tossed up on the shore!"

Snapping her mouth closed, Tammy swallowed hard. "How... how do you know my husband's name?" *And how did you know what I was praying...*

The girl grinned at her. "To answer your second question first, I know what the prayer was because Abba told me what you prayed. It's one of the reasons He sent me." Tammy forced her mouth to remain closed at that and willed her eyes to remain in their sockets.

"And I know Nathan's name just like I know yours, Tamara Elaine Rogers Diamond," she added with a grin.

Tammy gave up trying to control her body parts.

The girl's humor lightened a bit as she seemed to take pity on Tammy, reaching over the seat to grab her hand. It was unfathomable how she could do such a thing, though, since her arm would have had to be four feet long to reach across the space. Tammy stared at the hand covering her own. It looked normal enough, even had a little dirt under the nails. But nothing about this female was normal, as far as she could tell.

"I should introduce myself," she continued, her deep blue eyes twinkling. "I go by Chrissy. Or Chris." Tammy looked back up to see the girl shrug. "Lots of names, actually, depending on how I'm appearing to humans."

Uh... humans?

Chrissy grinned. "The look on your face is hilarious." She waved with the hand that had been covering Tammy's. "But never mind that. I was sent to give you some encouragement. To help out where I can. And to tell you that Abba is very happy that you've returned to Him," she said with a soft smile. "He truly loves when the prodigals come home. And it gives us angels a chance to burst out in song. I'm a danged good baritone, by the way."

Tammy's mouth was back to flopping. "An... an... angel?"

Another grin lit up Chrissy's face it was then that Tammy noticed she was glowing. Not a real brightness, like a lamp or anything, but it was as if a soft light surrounded her. Like a shining aura. She blinked a few times, but nothing changed.

Chrissy winked at her. "Yep. In the flesh." She glanced down at her body. "Well, sort of."

Tammy blinked some more. "But... but I thought... I thought angels were male."

That earned her a laugh. "We are... and we aren't. But for all intents and purposes, yeah, we're male." She shrugged. "We can appear however we want to— within certain limits—when we're in the earthly realm." She swept a hand to indicate her body.

"This is what I choose most often when I appear to Americans. It's the most... approachable."

Tammy nodded, still dumbfounded. She swallowed hard a few times and asked the Lord for some confirmation about this... woman's claims. Chrissy tilted her head and then laughed again.

"I am who I say I am," she said with a deep male voice that was so startling and disconnected with the body in front of her that Tammy huffed out a laugh.

"Okay, I... uh, I guess I believe you." She glanced at Nate again, who looked like he was dead, he was so still. That thought made her swallow hard and she blinked rapidly to stop the sudden moisture in her eyes from accumulating.

Chrissy reached out that extra-long arm again and patted her on the shoulder. "Everything will be okay," she told her. "You don't need to worry. The Lord has you in His hands." She smiled at Tammy with such a kind look that Tammy felt her throat close again. She nodded in response.

"Now, back to the first prayer... when you were questioning the Lord's return." She wagged a finger. "Don't ever doubt the Scripture, young lady."

That caused another laugh to escape Tammy. Chrissy appeared to be a good ten years younger than herself, though if she/he was an angel, then she was actually older than Tammy could even fathom.

Tammy shook her head. "I wasn't doubting Scripture... just, uh, my understanding of it, I guess."

Chrissy nodded. "People have gotten a lot of things wrong over the centuries. But on this point, you're questioning the fact that the Lord didn't take His people away before the craziness started, eh?" Tammy nodded and Chrissy smiled.

"Well, like I said at first, He *is* going to return for His people. Before the final judgment, before the last trumpet, all believers who remain will be taken up. The final judgment is not for you." Chrissy gave her what looked to be a sad smile. "Unfortunately, too many have decided that it's not going to happen, and they've given up. Given up on God." She shook her head.

"Just because a foretelling doesn't happen exactly the way people think it will, doesn't mean it isn't happening at all. That's where faith comes in. If the Lord says it's going to happen, you can bet it will."

Tammy nodded again, feeling a bit foolish for not contributing anything intelligent to the conversation. Chrissy nodded at the Bible on the seat next to her. "You just keep reading that and praying—*especially* praying—and everything will be just fine." She stood then and Tammy stared up, rather shocked to see what she thought was a small woman was really about six feet tall.

The angel smiled again. "I have to leave now. Abba's got me going in all sorts of directions with different missions, but I'll be back." She nodded toward Nate.

"Hopefully the next time we meet, your husband won't get his panties in a wad because you're talking to angels."

Tammy barked out a surprised laugh at the angel's words, then with a wink, Chrissy was just... gone.

Tammy stared at the empty space where the angel had been for a long time, to the point she started thinking she'd hallucinated the whole thing. Doubt crept in, making her wonder if she'd gotten too hot in the train car, if she was suffering from heat exhaustion. It would explain a lot of things, because...

"Are they not all ministering spirits, sent out to render service for the sake of those who will inherit salvation?"

The voice—that she knew without a doubt now was truly the Lord's—startled her out of her questions and doubts. She grinned.

"Thanks, Father," she whispered. Nate snorted on a snore and lifted his head.

"What was that?" he slurred, sleepiness coloring his words.

Tammy laughed; her husband had slept through a loud, laughing angel visitation, but startled awake at her tiny whisper. She smiled over at him.

"Nothing, honey. Go back to sleep."

He shook his head as he sat up, rubbing his face with both hands. Nate blinked a few times, looking around the train car. Then he rubbed his eyes and yawned.

"Nah, I'm awake now," he said. Tammy didn't think he looked very awake, but she kept her thoughts to herself. He looked at her with a frown. "I had the weirdest dream," he said, tilting his head as if trying to remember it all.

"What was it about?"

Nate shook his head. "It was—there was this girl..." He shook his head again, then reached for his backpack and pulled out a bottle of water. He uncapped it and took a sip, then offered the bottle to her.

"Never mind," he said, "it was too crazy to repeat."

Let me guess... you dreamed of a little blonde who was really an angel? Tammy wanted to laugh, but she bit her lips. She knew they'd see Chrissy again and couldn't wait to see Nate's reaction when his "dream" showed up.

They had a light meal, sharing one of the prepackaged meals they'd gotten at Gerald's. Tammy thought it was funny how she'd dieted most of her adult life and had never been very successful, except for the really strict diet she'd put herself on before their wedding. But now that they were walking so much and eating so little, she knew she was underweight. They both were.

Once it grew dark once again, Nate moved to the train car door. Tammy sighed as she picked up her backpack, not looking forward to another long walk. She wished they could just hang out in the train car for a few days, but she knew that her husband wanted to get to their destination as soon as they could. He was on a life-or-death time schedule.

She swallowed at the lump in her throat, but then remembered the angel's words: *Everything will be okay. You don't need to worry. The Lord has you in His hands.*

While Nate's reason for rushing to get to Felicia's father's "community, she knew the angel's words were true. And she also knew with just as much assurance that her husband wouldn't rest until he knew that she was safe.

Tammy loved him for it but wished he wouldn't push himself so hard. While she was struggling physically after a lifetime of little to no exercise, she knew that Nate—who had always been in great shape—was struggling even more. Every step seemed to be harder and harder for him.

She stepped off the train car and walked silently behind her husband as they headed south once more. He'd said that they'd have to go "off road" over the next several weeks, and Tammy hoped that they would find some abandoned house to stay in. Hopefully one with running water. And soap.

Nate tripped over some unseen object and Tammy automatically reached out to grab his arm. He violently yanked away from her, snarling, "I don't need your help!"

She jerked her hand away, shocked. Knowing of her past, Nate had never acted like that with her. In fact, he rarely lost his temper enough to even raise his voice, careful to not cause any of her PTSD symptoms to resurface.

Swallowing hard, she mumbled an apology as she slowed her steps so that she was a few paces behind him once again.

It was a long while later before he spoke again, after pausing to wait for her to catch up. He didn't comment on the fact that she'd been lagging behind. The more she'd fretted over his actions, the slower her steps had become, to the point she'd dropped back a dozen or more yards.

Nate pointed to a field. "I think this is where we need to cross." He pulled the map closer to his face and squinted at it in the pale moonlight. Tammy had been so caught up in her thoughts that she hadn't even noticed he'd pulled it out. She had no idea how he knew where they were on the map, other than the road they'd been following, but she had to trust that Nate knew where they were heading. She was a terrible navigator herself and had always joked that she couldn't even find her way out of the mall.

Nate didn't apologize for his earlier behavior and Tammy decided to just let it go. He was probably just as tired of walking as she was, plus he put the added stress on himself of worrying about their situation, while she was learning to lean on the Lord more and more. And now, knowing that He actually sent one of His angels just to talk to her... she was having a hard time worrying or being upset about anything, honestly.

As they started across a field that looked like it had once grown corn, Tammy prayed that the Lord would help her be more understanding of her husband's moods, that He would help her be patient and kind. She also asked for help in dealing with her PTSD, since she hadn't been able to see her therapist in over six months.

But that was before she'd gotten right with the Lord once again, since she'd "returned home," as Chrissy had put it. Tammy knew that, even with seeing the therapist every week, if Nate had acted the way he had earlier back then, she would have had a full-blown panic attack and would have shut down for a long time.

It seemed the Lord was a much better counselor than any human therapist, she thought to herself with a smile.

They trudged across the field for a long time, both tripping over the unseen, their steps faltering when their feet met with hidden holes. Tammy prayed again that they would get through their journey without injury.

That made her think of her leg, which she knew the Lord Himself had healed. If she hadn't prayed for the healing, she had no doubt that it would have been a lot worse and would have likely gotten infected. Jesus was the Great Physician, after all, and she'd told Nate that on several occasions.

Nate had chosen to grab first-aid supplies at Gerald's, rather than trust in the Lord.

She sighed at her thoughts, wondering if her

husband was ever going to give his life to Christ. He was certainly stubborn and opinionated when it came to anything to do with religion of any kind and Tammy blamed his parents for that.

Nate rarely spoke to them any longer, since they always came down on him for marrying a "shiksa." When Nate's father had called her that name the first time they'd met, she'd asked her husband what it meant, but he would never tell her. She'd finally looked it up on the internet and had been heartbroken to discover it was highly derogatory. Basically, a curse word for a Gentile woman.

That was the first and last time she'd gone with Nate to his parents'. He himself stopped going after their first year of marriage.

But Tammy also knew that no one was beyond redemption. She'd read many stories of hardened criminals who'd given their lives to Christ, many while in prison. If a demon-possessed prostitute could be saved, then she figured even her hard-hearted, hard-headed husband could. And so could his Christian-hating parents.

"We'll stop soon," Nate murmured, bringing her out of her thoughts. Tammy looked up, startled to see that the glow of dawn was already on the horizon. Usually by that time, her feet and legs were aching so much that she didn't think she could take another step. She wondered if she was just getting in better shape, or if the Lord was helping her along. Either way, she was grateful for it.

"Where?" she asked as she came up behind him. Nate stopped and spun around to face her and she nearly bumped into him.

"Why do you always have to question me?" he

snarled. "You never trust me to just take care of things!" He spoke much louder than he usually did and once again, Tammy took a step back in fear, her heart pounding at the strange man in front of her.

She began to wonder if he had gotten possessed himself.

Nate stepped toward her, fists clenched at his sides. "I swear, I'm sick and tired of it, of you, of everything!" When he took another step, Tammy hastily took two more back. Her foot caught on something, and she fell hard. Pain shot up her back and she cried out.

Her usually gentle, loving husband sneered at her as he stood over her, then turned on his heel and stomped off. Tammy remained where she was, staring after him in shock.

What in the world is wrong with him?

Wincing at the pain in her back, she rolled over and forced herself onto her hands and knees, then slowly pushed up to a stand. Her hands were stinging as well, and she held them up, trying to see if they were injured. It was hard to tell in the low light, but she carefully dusted them off, thankful that she didn't feel any wetness to indicate blood.

"What's wrong?"

She jumped at the sound of her husband's voice so close. She hadn't even noticed him coming back and she stared at him with wide eyes, wondering if he was going to turn into Mr. Hyde once again. He was looking at her with concern on his face and Tammy felt no small amount of confusion.

"You saw me fall," she said, accusation in her voice. "I hurt my back and my hands are stinging."

She looked back at her palms.

Nate stepped closer and Tammy couldn't help but flinch. That caused him to frown in confusion. "What's wrong with you?" he asked. "You know I'd never hurt you." The tone of his voice indicated *he* was hurt by her actions.

Tammy made a dismissive sound. "I don't know that," she snapped. "Not with the way you've been acting tonight."

Nate's frown deepened. "What do you mean?"

Her mouth dropped open in disbelief. He knew all about her past, all about the abuse and fears that she'd worked so hard to get past. Nate knew every single trigger she had, yet he'd managed to flip several of them in just a few hours. But the man seemed genuinely confused, so she just shook her head, telling herself he was probably just exhausted and not thinking right.

"Never mind," she muttered. "Let's find shelter before the sun comes up." She brushed past him, walking carefully, as every step jarred her back.

Nate fell into step beside her. "Wait up," he said, putting a hand on her arm. Tammy huffed but stopped. She flinched again when he reached out to gently take the backpack off her shoulders and she moaned. The relief she felt at having that heavy thing off while her back muscles were tightening more with each step was tangible.

He pushed one of the straps up over his shoulder and Tammy felt a moment of guilt at all the weight he was now carrying. But that thought left as quickly as it came; as far as she was concerned, it was his fault she'd been hurt in the first place.

"I saw a building not too far ahead," he told her as they started walking again. She didn't respond as she noticed that he kept his pace slow to accommodate her. As soon as they were stopped for the day, she was going to have it out with the man. Being nice to her after being such a jerk wasn't going to solve the problems. She was going to set some firm boundaries.

They walked in silence for maybe ten more minutes when Nate motioned for her to move into a cluster of trees. She did as he instructed, then watched as he took off the packs before slinking around toward the building to check it out. It was just a few moments when he came back.

"Deserted," he told her as he picked up the packs and motioned with his head for her to follow. *Like you have to tell me,* she thought with an eye roll.

Nate had to break a window, which made Tammy wince; she hated the thought of destroying someone's property. But she also knew that the times they were in called for some desperate measures occasionally. She just prayed that the owners were long gone and wouldn't even know they'd broken in.

She waited by the door while Nate climbed through the window, not speaking as she walked by him when he opened the door. After closing it, he looked at her, that same confused look on his face.

"What's wrong?" he asked again.

It was her turn to frown. "Not here," she told him. "Let's figure out where we're gonna sleep and then we'll have it out." With that, she turned and examined their surroundings.

The house was obviously deserted. Though she grimaced at the dust and dirt covering every surface, she also felt better about the broken window. The owners—if they were still among the living—hadn't been there for a very long time.

Surprisingly, the house was sparsely furnished with a small sofa and end table in what was apparently the living room to the right of the entryway. She noticed some pictures on the fireplace mantle and walked over to look at them.

Typical family pictures lined the shelf—black and white photos of a young couple with two small children standing in front of a car and others of the same couple, though much younger, on their wedding day. From the looks of the pictures, they were taken in the early fifties, or sixties.

The age of the photographs decreased with each one, telling a lifetime of stories. The young couple aging, the children growing up and having children of their own, family get-togethers at holidays. The last picture on the mantle was of a very elderly couple hugging, with the man kissing his woman on the temple. It was such a sweet photograph it made Tammy's throat tighten with emotion.

She'd always hoped that she and Nate could end their lives like that—still in love and devoted to one another despite the years and the mileage. But she knew that wasn't going to happen. Even if they could work out their problems, there just wasn't the time to grow old.

Everything was coming to an end.

A heavy sigh lifted her shoulders and she turned to find Nate staring at her, an unreadable look on his face. She knew he wanted to know what was on her mind, but she wasn't in the mood to discuss it, not before she'd told him she wasn't going to put up with his verbal attacks.

"C'mon," she murmured. "Let's figure out where we're gonna sleep."

Nate pulled one of his guns out and motioned for her to stay at the bottom of the stairs while he went upstairs to check the area first, but she was tired of staying behind. Playing the "helpless little woman" was starting to get on her nerves and instead of waiting, she silently followed after him.

Her husband turned right at the top of the stairs, so Tammy turned left. He still hadn't noticed her, which she thought was a little strange. Nate was always very alert and could rarely be startled. It made her frown, thinking of all the ways he'd been acting differently. She was no longer so sure it was just stress causing it.

Early morning light was streaming in through a half-circle window at the end of the hall, revealing most of the doors were closed. Tammy thought that was a bit strange, but she moved to the last room on the right and opened the door, peeking in.

It was completely empty, though there were a few crumpled papers on the floor and some rather large dust bunnies in the corners. Dark squares and rectangles on the blue walls silently proclaimed pictures and posters once hung there. It looked like it was probably a boy's room and Tammy wondered which one of the young men in the pictures on the mantle had occupied the space.

The next room was a craft room—dust covered thread spools perched on tiny pegs lining one shelf, with baby food jars on the shelf above containing colorful buttons, sequins and the like. A large table was pushed against one wall, scissors and a dress pattern still atop it. There wasn't a sewing machine, but there was a workstation where one had probably

100

been at one time.

Another door revealed a bathroom. No water was in the commode and Tammy tried flushing it, not surprised when nothing happened. She left the door open and moved to the room across the hall.

It was another bedroom, this one obviously occupied by a girl at one time. The decor theme seemed to be unicorns and rainbows and it made Tammy smile to see it. Purples and pinks in every shade imaginable were so prevalent, it was almost nauseating.

Judging by the pictures, the children had grown up in the house and she wondered why a teenage girl would have chosen such a theme. *Maybe the grandparents had helped raise a grandchild or two.* She pondered the circumstances that could have made that a necessity.

She laughed at her thoughts; her imagination was running away with her. "What does it matter anyway," she muttered to herself. "It's not like we're gonna be living here."

The bedroom had a bed, though it was the type that could be made into a sofa. *A day bed, I think.* She laughed to herself at the thought of she and Nate trying to share the tiny thing. It was even smaller than the twin bed they'd slept in back at the cellar. She hoped one of the other bedrooms had something bigger.

Tammy frowned when she got closer to the bed. The southwestern bedspread with tribal patterns didn't fit the girly decor, which she supposed wasn't so odd. But what was strange was the bed looked... fresh. Where everything else in the house was dusty looking, the bed covers were almost clean appearing. And it looked like it had been recently slept in.

She gnawed at her lip as she pondered it, wondering how long it had been since someone had been in the house. The other rooms hadn't been used, there hadn't been water in the toilet... she tilted her head. There had been a bucket next to the toilet that she hadn't really thought much of, but now it triggered a memory.

A construction crew laying a new sewer had accidentally cut into the water line on their block a few years back. She and Nate and their neighbors had been without water for three days. The city had a water delivery service come to the neighborhood and they'd used five-gallon jugs for drinking and the like until the line had been repaired. And one of the things they'd had to do was pour water into the toilet bowl to get it to flush.

The house she was standing in was in the middle of nowhere, a farmhouse centered on surrounding acreage that had probably been cornfields or the like at one time. It wasn't like water would be easy to come by. Someone would have to haul it from a great distance if there wasn't a well.

Or electricity to operate a pump.

She moved to the window. The shadows were long on that side of the house, the sun's light just starting to warm the day. Now that she could see more clearly, Tammy realized she'd been right; there wasn't another house anywhere in sight. In fact, the only other structure for miles around was the barn that sat probably twenty yards from the house.

It was very remote, an unlikely place to come across others. She felt a pang of longing, wishing they could stay there at the farm with the ghosts of happy memories lingering in the atmosphere.

The rays of the morning sun cleared the northeast corner of the house just then and Tammy stared down into the yard, half expecting to see abandoned tricycles and toy dump trucks. Instead, something more interesting caught her eye.

An old-fashioned water pump, the kind you had to pump by hand. *The kind that works without electricity.* And there was another plastic bucket sitting next to it.

She frowned again; the house had obviously been abandoned for many years, yet there were clean-looking covers on the little daybed in the girl's room. There was a bucket next to the toilet in the bathroom and now another one down below. She wondered what the odds were that a bucket—plastic, nonetheless—could have withstood the weather for so many years, and especially the spring winds prevalent in the area. The thing would have blown into Kentucky by now.

Tammy sighed; there wasn't any sign of anyone living in the house now and she supposed whoever had been staying there had moved on. She wondered if it could have even been Gerald and Felicia who'd stopped for a little while, resting on their long journey to Florida. She hoped so, while at the same time envying them if they had. She would have loved to camp at the charming house for about a week.

She turned from the window when she heard a shuffling sound. Nate must have been in the hall and knew he'd be surprised when he saw her standing there. She hoped he didn't shoot her unintentionally.

It wasn't Nate that she saw, though and the breath whooshed out of her.

"Oh..."

Chapter 6

ATHAN WAS getting frustrated. More so by each passing moment. The house seemed to be empty, but for some reason he couldn't shake the feeling that he was being watched.

With each door he opened, his frustration mounted. Agitation was making him feel twitchy, the muscle tremors causing his limbs to jerk. He realized it was getting out of hand, to the point he was losing his balance. He forced himself to take deep breaths to try to calm himself, much like Tammy did when she felt an impending panic attack.

It didn't help.

A low growl surprised him, and he whirled around, aiming his weapon. Fully expecting to see a dog behind him, he frowned when he saw there wasn't anything in the hall. He turned and looked in the bedroom he'd been about to investigate, but it was completely empty. There wasn't even a stick of furniture for something— or someone—to hide behind.

Closing the door, he looked out the half circle window at the end of the hall to see that the sun had fully breached the horizon. He squinted into the brightness, angry that it was so late already. He needed to make sure the house was empty, and then find a place where he and Tammy could get some rest.

Thinking about that also made him angry. The idea that everything was falling on his shoulders was just too much at times. He didn't want to be in charge, didn't want to lead them to wherever it was they were going. The map Gerald had left behind had a path to follow, but it ended somewhere near Tallahassee and he was sure that Felicia's father lived in the Keys. He just knew they were going to get all the way to the Gulf and then be stuck.

That thought made him want to put his fist through the wall.

Taking some more deep breaths helped a little bit, as did the small voice in the back of his mind telling him that he didn't need to be in charge, that Tammy was his wife, not his subordinate. He argued with the voice, telling it that he was the only one with any kind of survival instincts and that his wife had zero skills whatsoever when it came to defending herself. She had no sense of self-preservation either. The woman just charged into situations without thinking.

Another growl caught his attention and he spun around, once again finding an empty hall. It was then he realized he was the one growling.

Wondering at that strangeness, he shook it off as he opened another door, this one revealing a bathroom. He turned the faucet and wasn't surprised when no water came out. A sigh lifted his shoulders when he knew Tammy would be complaining about not being able to take a bath or shower.

He growled once again.

Just before he turned to leave, something beside the toilet caught his eye. It was a bucket, one of the five-gallon plastic types the home improvement places sold. Or used to, anyway. Nearly all the stores had shut down after the crash. All that was left were small mom and pop type places that dealt mostly in trades.

It was another reason he felt like they needed to leave their town—they had nothing left to trade with.

Nathan's hands clenched at his sides as the anger

crept back up. Truly, he just wanted to tear something apart. Or, better yet, beat the tar out of someone.

He shook his head, knowing he wasn't thinking clearly. If he were being honest with himself, he knew that he hadn't been thinking right for several days. He also knew it was part of his disease, which meant it was progressing faster than he'd hoped. It made him even more desperate to get to the commune or whatever it was Gerald told them to go to.

But no... he thought to himself, the inner voice sneering in sarcasm. *We have to stop and rest. Always resting. Tammy can't walk more than a few miles without her feet hurting. Or having to take a leak. Freaking woman drives me crazy...*

Nathan closed his eyes at his thoughts and sucked in some more air. He loved Tammy, he reminded himself, had loved her since they'd met at the police station her first day on the job as a dispatcher. His thoughts toward her now weren't right. Weren't accurate. And he needed to get them under control before he did something he'd regret.

He looked back at the bucket, forcing his thoughts to remain on the present situation. It made him think that someone must have been in the house after the owners had either died or fled. No water, no toilets flushing. Coupled with the feeling of being watched he'd had several times while searching the upstairs, Nathan had a suspicion there were others about.

A sound caught his attention then and he whirled around to investigate. The doors in the hall had been closed, but now he saw that one was open. He lifted his handgun and held it with both hands as he slid along the wall. He hadn't done such a thing in a long time, ever since he'd been forced to leave the force. Anger bubbled up again at that thought, but he shoved it back down.

As he approached the doorway, he frowned when he saw his wife. *The stupid woman can never do as she's told!* He nearly growled again, but he caught himself in time. Tammy was staring at something, her back to the window, and Nathan knew he might need to keep the element of surprise.

Though the house was old, the floors weren't creaky as would be expected. He peeked through the crack where the door hinges met the frame but couldn't see what Tammy was looking at. Or who.

"Are you alone?" his wife asked. *Okay, so it's a "who."*

There wasn't an answer, but Nathan assumed whoever it was shook their head... or nodded, because Tammy then asked, "Who's with you?"

Still no answer. Nathan had to assume that whoever she was talking to wasn't hostile, because she didn't seem upset. In fact, she was keeping her voice soft, like she was speaking to a child.

He stepped into the doorway, making himself known.

Sure enough, a small girl was standing in the doorway of a closet, thumb in mouth and clutching what looked like a bundle of rags. She was filthy, and her hair was a mass of mats and tangles. Her eyes never left Tammy, though, and Nathan thought she was looking at his wife like she was some kind of savior.

"Everything okay?" he asked as he walked into the room, tucking the gun into the back of his waistband. The little girl's head whipped around, eyes wide as she let out a little scream, then spun around back into the closet, slamming the door behind her.

Seconds later, two more children ran into the room.

Nathan quickly assessed them: an older boy, maybe twelve and a girl who might have been eight or nine. Both were in as bad of shape as the little girl and were so thin, they looked like a stiff breeze would blow them into the next county. Nathan felt a pinch in his chest that he couldn't identify.

The boy swallowed hard as he looked between Tammy and Nathan, then he glanced at the girl, who Nathan assumed was his sister.

"Uh, this is our house," he said, his voice squeaking in a tell-tale sign of puberty. Nathan hadn't thought the boy was that old, but with the near starvation it was possible he was a lot older than he appeared.

"It was our GG's house," he added.

"GG?" Tammy asked with that soft voice again. It was aggravating, Nathan thought. Almost a sing-song thing that made him want to tell her to shut up. He blinked several times at the thought; he'd never said anything unkind like that to his wife, not once. He worried about how far along the disease was, if he was having such bad mood swings already.

We need to hurry to Florida. These delays are ridiculous! He forced himself to unclench his fists.

"Great-gramma," the boy explained. The little girl sidled closer to him and he wrapped a protective arm around her shoulders. Nathan wondered again if they were siblings. They looked nothing alike, though. The boy had dark hair, and the girl had what looked like might be strawberry blonde, though it was hard to tell through the filth.

"Oh," Tammy said softly. "Are they the older couple in the pictures on the fireplace?" Both children nodded.

"They died," the boy shrugged.

Nathan didn't have the patience for the conversation. Who cared whose house it was? All he wanted to know is if there were other adults around—someone he might have to shoot. Or, better yet, punch. His fists clenched in anticipation before he could stop himself.

He shook away the thoughts once again.

"Where're your parents?" Tammy asked before he could. He really wanted to shake the information out of the boy, but the saner part of him knew that wasn't the right thing to do. He tried to cling to that voice of reason, but it seemed to be no more than a wisp of smoke, a vapor that dissolved with the tiniest of breezes.

"Dead too," the boy said, shrugging again. Tammy made a noise of distress and Nathan knew she was going to go on and on with sympathetic words. He didn't want to waste the time letting her do so.

"Are you with anyone else?" he said, his voice little more than the growl that had escaped him earlier. Both of the kids' eyes widened as they stared at him and shook their heads.

"Just Sissy," the boy said, pointing to the closet. "This was her room when we stayed with GG." He shrugged again. "Our rooms got cleaned out. Think the neighbors stole the beds and stuff."

"Neighbors?" Tammy asked. Nathan again had the urge to tell her to shut up, that he was the one who should be questioning the suspects. She was just a civilian.

The little voice told him that the kids weren't suspects... and that he and Tammy were *both* civilians.

He ignored it.

The boy pointed toward the window. "Yeah, Nelsons across the west pasture. Can't see the house, but they're on the other side of the tree line." He made a face. "They're thieves. GG always said so. Said she had to watch her cows and chickens, 'else the Nelsons would take 'em."

"Oh no," Tammy said in that idiotic voice again. Nathan glared at her, trying to silently will her to stop talking, but she didn't even look his way. That made him even angrier.

The boy pointed his thumb at his chest. "I'm Carl and this here's Lou," he said, jerking his head at the girl beside him. "Sissy, get out here!" he hollered then in the direction of the closet. Nathan turned to see the knob turn and then the door opened a crack. Slowly, so slowly that he wanted to stomp over and shove the door open, the little girl opened the door and peered out with wide, terrified looking eyes.

I'll give you a reason to be afraid...

That thought made him jerk upright so violently that the others looked at him in question. He had to shake his head once again; never in his life had he hurt a child—or a woman, for that matter. In fact, he had been known for being the "sweet cop," a title that had been given to him by Missus Delaney after he'd gone to the grocery store for her when she'd hurt her knee. The other officers had loved teasing him about that one.

The fact that he was now wanting to yell at his wife and frighten little children was concerning, to say the least. Even more so when he realized that he seemed to be losing control over his emotions faster and faster.

A few more deep breaths helped calm him. He closed his eyes, as well, because the little girl was staring at him like he was about to lose it. Nathan supposed that was a fair assessment.

"It's okay," Tammy said in a coaxing voice that grated on his nerves. *More deep breaths.* "We're not gonna hurt you."

Hopefully.

The child named "Sissy," of all things—and Nathan thought that was a really stupid name, though he didn't voice that opinion—took a hesitant step, then another. When no one pounced on her, she darted over to her brother, who wrapped his other arm around her. Nathan snorted; *like that scarecrow could do anything to stop me...*

"Sorry you got stuck in here," Carl murmured to his little sister, who darted a glance up at him and gave a slight nod, though her thumb never left her mouth.

"How about we go down to the dining room and see what we can find to eat?" Tammy suggested. Carl and Lou both shook their heads.

"Ain't nothing to eat here," Carl said with such a forlorn voice that Nathan almost felt sorry for the kid.

"Well, Nate and I have food," his wife said. Nathan looked at her sharply, furious that she was offering to share what precious little they had. He wasn't sure they even had enough food to get them to the coast as it was. He managed to keep his thoughts to himself, though, even when Tammy returned his glare with one of her own, as if daring him to say something.

He grumbled to himself as he followed the others down the stairs and into the dining room. There was an old oak table and chairs, one that had seen better years. As they sat while Tammy got the backpacks, Nathan noticed the tabletop had names carved all over it. He wondered who in their right mind would let someone carve their name into the dining table.

"GG wanted all the kids to put their names on here when they got old enough," Carl said, obviously noticing where Nathan's attention was. "We all did it, 'cept Sissy, cuz she ain't old enough yet."

Tammy returned with the backpacks and started pulling out the freeze-dried meals. She opened three packs and then a water bottle, pouring a little into each tray section to reconstitute the food. Nathan hated the meals, but it was better than nothing. Which is what there was—nothing.

While the food was rehydrating, she went into the kitchen and open and closed drawers until she found forks. Once the kids had their utensils, she handed each of them a meal.

They ate all of it within a minute or less. Even Sissy.

"Wow, you guys must have been really hungry," Tammy said as she pulled out one of the packs of trail mix they'd taken from Gerald's. She handed it to Nathan, who stared at it like it was something detestable. He wanted a meal too and was about to say something, but Tammy shot him another look. He narrowed his eyes back at her. She ignored him as she looked back at the kids.

"When was the last time you ate?"

Carl shrugged. Nathan noticed that the girls hadn't spoken a single word yet, which he found strange. Most females wanted to talk your ears off. Well, except Tammy. That woman was almost as closed-lipped as he was, he thought.

"Think it was maybe three days ago," the kid said.

"Oh my," Tammy breathed. "Well, we have plenty of food to share—"

"We do not!" Nathan said as he hit the table, scattering his trail mix. The girls cringed and the littlest one shot out of her chair and slid under the table. He turned to glare at Tammy, who had a shocked look on her face.

"We barely have enough for ourselves!" he protested. "We can't be feeding every stray dog we come across," he finished with a growl.

His wife's eyes narrowed as a murderous look came over her. Nathan's eyebrows rose at that; he didn't remember ever seeing such an expression from her before. He might have crossed a line, but he couldn't find it in himself to care.

"We have more than enough food to feed the children," she said in a deceptively soft voice. "And what we need, the Lord will provide."

Nathan couldn't help the derisive sound that left his lips. "Yeah, right," he grumbled, but he didn't argue any further. Tammy stared at him for a moment longer, then turned back to the kids. She bent sideways to look under the table.

"It's okay, Sissy. Nate might sound scary, but he's really not. He would never hurt you." She lifted her head slightly to give him a look that said *You better not.* He curled his lip at her in response.

It took a few moments of coaxing and Nathan was just about to yell, "Just yank her out!" when the little girl finally crawled out of her own accord. She turned those big, blue terrified eyes to him once again, then moved to stand next to Carl, who wrapped his arm around his little sister again while glaring at Nathan.

Nathan had to hand it to the kid for having the guts to do so.

Remorse suddenly swamped over him, so much so that he felt tears pricking at the back of his eyes. *What the heck?* He never cried. Never. Blinking furiously, he turned to stare at the tabletop once again.

He felt so guilty for having treated the kids so rottenly. What kind of a monster did such a thing? he wondered. It was crazy, and certainly not like him. The kids were half-starved orphans, for Pete's sake. They needed help, not some crazy person spitting poisonous barbs at them. *It has to be the disease,* he told himself once again.

Nathan cleared his throat. "I'm sorry," he murmured. "I... I'm... uh..." he huffed out a frustrated breath and forced himself to look at the kids, wet eyes or not. They deserved to see how sorry he was.

"I'm not usually like that," he tried to explain, waving his hand. "Angry. Scary," he added with a smile for Sissy. The poor thing was still staring at him like he might eat her at any moment. It made him suck in a shuddering breath, trying to get a grip on his emotions. Nothing seemed to be helping.

His shoulders slumped in defeat. There was nothing he could say to take back the fact that he'd terrified the poor, innocent children. Children who had done nothing wrong. They were just trying to survive themselves...

Nathan's thoughts caused him to suck in a sob and he covered his face with both hands. It was just a moment later when he felt a hand on his back and knew it was Tammy. She rubbed circles on his shoulder blade.

"It's okay, honey," she said soothingly. "I know you're having a hard time right now. Is it the stress? The worry?" He shook his head while keeping his hands over his face.

"What is it?" she asked. She sounded so worried, so bewildered, that Nate's eyes filled even more. He'd caused his wife to worry needlessly. He'd probably scared her, as well, though she'd done a very good job of hiding it. In fact, she'd stood right up to him.

"I'm just... so sorry..." he sobbed again, both embarrassed and feeling genuine remorse. He was having a very difficult time sorting his emotions.

Tammy continued to rub his back as she put her hand on his thigh. She murmured soothing words, "It's okay. It'll be all right." It didn't help, not really, but just the fact that she was willing to forgive him made him sob even harder.

He felt a hand on his other thigh then, and he parted his hands enough to see little Sissy staring up at him, thumb in mouth, hair impossibly matted, big, blue eyes that held a world of pain in their depths. Nathan gave her a wobbly smile, then choked as he thought of how much the little thing had gone through. And how he'd added to her pain.

It was a long while before he felt like he was in control enough to function. He took a few deep breaths, then nodded to Tammy with a grateful smile. Sissy continued petting his leg like he was a frightened animal needing comfort, and Nathan supposed that was exactly what he was to her. An animal. He'd treated her like a grizzly bear with a burr in its paw, yet the little angel was willing to forgive him.

Before that thought caused another round of unmanly tears, he cleared his throat and swallowed hard. He smiled again at Sissy, then looked back at the other children, who were staring at him like he was the craziest thing they'd ever seen.

"I, uh, have a... I'm sick," he hedged. "It's hard to explain, but it makes me a little... well, a little crazy, I guess. Just started the past day or so with the anger, which you saw. And now this," he said with an embarrassed laugh as he waved at his face that felt puffy and hot.

He held out his right hand, letting the kids see the tremor that had become continuous. It never stopped, and his leg was getting worse as well.

"Causes that too," he said. "Shaking."

"Is there medicine you can take?" Carl asked, though he directed the question at Tammy. Nathan figured the boy thought he was too crazy to answer for himself. He was probably right about that.

Tammy shook her head. "No, there isn't," she said, a sad note in her voice. It made Nathan think of her being alone, having to deal with the world's insanity on her own. He had to clear his throat against the emotion once again.

"But we can pray for Nate," she said. There was a brightness in her voice, and he noticed the kids seemed to perk up at the suggestion as well. He wanted to tell them no, he didn't want them to pray for him, but at the same time he didn't want to hurt their feelings.

"We used to pray all the time with Gramma Rose," Carl said. "She liked goin' to church."

Tammy smiled at him. "Is that the one you call GG?"

Carl shook his head. "Nah, that's Great-Gramma Lizzie. Rose was—" he tilted his head, as if in thought. "She was GG's daughter, I think. Mighta been dad's mama though." He shrugged. "Not sure."

"She's dead too?" Tammy asked. Carl and Lou both nodded their heads.

"Yeah. The whole family's dead," the boy answered, matter-of-factly.

Nathan wondered at that, at how a young boy such as Carl could come to be so nonchalant over something so horrendous. Losing their family had to be traumatic, but the kid just acted like it was an everyday occurrence.

"How did you come to be here?" Tammy asked. "In this house, I mean."

Carl glanced at Lou. The older girl looked away with a shrug. It seemed to give him the permission he sought.

"We had to leave our... uh, the foster family we were with." He glanced at his sister again, but she was staring at the table, her finger tracing over a carving. Nathan squinted, seeing that the name was "Rick." He wondered if that might have been their father.

His chest ached again.

Tammy seemed to realize that the topic was a sore one. Of course, anyone would have noticed that the kids all had a stricken look, even little Sissy, who was still patting Nathan's thigh. He gave her a soft smile,

118

then reached out to pat her on the back, but she gave a little shriek, then darted back under the table. In just a few seconds, she was standing next to her brother once again.

Carl glanced down at Sissy, wrapping that protective arm around her once more. He looked back at Nathan with a sad smile. "She, uh, don't like to be touched." He nodded toward Lou.

"Her either. At least, not by men." He looked at Tammy. "You'll prob'ly be okay though."

Nathan's eyes widened at the implications. Girls not wanting to be touched by men… The story might as well have been carved on the table with the names.

He was glad that his emotions had shifted to the blubbery type, because if he'd still been feeling the rage he had earlier, there was no telling what he might have done. Demanded names, addresses, then gone on a revenging rampage. Who knew what all. All he did know was it was a good thing he felt like crying for the children's circumstance at the moment.

Tammy gave a little sniffle and Nathan's chest constricted again. He knew it had to be hard on his wife, hearing that other children had suffered much as she had. There had been a time early in their marriage when Tammy had talked about going into the social work field, finishing her degree after switching majors. But both Nathan and her therapist had talked her out of it… at least until she'd gotten over the trauma of her childhood.

She never had.

Clearing his throat once again, he reached over and put his hand on top of Tammy's. She gave him a small, sad smile, but then cleared her own throat.

"So, you said there wasn't any food here?" she said a little too brightly as she changed the subject. Carl nodded.

Tammy motioned toward the kitchen. "There isn't a hidden pantry anywhere, is there?" Nathan chuckled at that, but Carl looked puzzled as he shook his head.

"Okay, well, guess we'll have to pray for Nathan *and* for the Lord to provide for us."

Her words caused Nathan to frown; not over the fact she wanted to pray for him, because she'd already said they were going to do so. What caused him to pause was the implication that she'd just made—that they were going to be taking care of the kids.

"Uh, honey, we can't stay here—"

Tammy interrupted him with a wave of her hand. "I know," she said, softening her words with a smile. "I know that you're in a hurry to get to Florida. We'll leave as soon as we're rested." As she said that, she stifled a yawn with a laugh.

Nathan frowned. "So, we're gonna leave all our food with the kids?" At that point, he was willing to do so. *The poor things, having to fend for themselves...* He straightened in his seat, telling himself to quit being such a sissy girl. That thought made him glance at the girl named Sissy who was sucking vigorously on her thumb. He smiled to himself, thinking of how accurate the colloquialism was.

Tammy shook her head, smiling again. "Nope. They're gonna come with us."

Chapter 7

THE KIDS didn't really want to leave what they considered to be their home, even if it had been their great-grandparents'. Tammy understood; it represented a place of safety.

It had taken a bit of convincing to get them to agree to leave, even though it was Carl who seemed to make the decisions. The girls were still uncommunicative and that was concerning. Tammy wondered exactly how much trauma they'd gone through.

She could imagine.

Once Nate had told Carl that they couldn't leave all the food with them, the kid had reluctantly agreed to go and had set about packing their belongings. It had broken Tammy's heart to see how little the kids had— one change of clothing each, the shoes they were wearing and only Sissy had any sort of toy, which was a very ratty rag doll.

While the kids packed, Nate went outside to refill their water bottles. Carl had told him that the old hand pump still worked, but the pipes were rusty and told him to let the water run for a few minutes before it would be drinkable. Both Nate and Tammy had been impressed with the kid's intelligence.

Since they hadn't had any sleep since the day before and the kids had been sleeping on a "normal" schedule, Nate and Tammy decided they'd stay awake for most of the day, taking just small catnaps before the sun went down.

After a short nap, Tammy busied herself with digging through cabinets and drawers, trying to see if there was anything useful they could take with them. It seemed most of the usable items had been taken—or stolen, as Carl had said—but she did manage to find an old-fashioned bottle opener that had a sharp point on one end. She seemed to remember seeing someone—maybe her father—use such a thing to poke a triangle-shaped hole in the top of a can. She also found a small manicure set and a few boxes of matches.

Tucking the items into her pocket, she moved to the drawer below. It was empty, but in the back was a slip of paper with numbers written on it. There was also a name that caught her eye—Pam T. Seller, though the "Pam" looked more like "Pan." Tammy stared at it for a moment, then laughed, wondering if it meant what she thought it might.

Pantry cellar.

The numbers did look like a combination, three two-digit numbers, though they were written like a phone number, with a zero at the end. Frowning, she wondered at the odds of discovering a clue to yet another hidden cellar, but then she shrugged, knowing that the Lord could have been going ahead of them, providing even before they'd need it.

Tammy went outside to talk to Nate about what she'd discovered. She showed him the paper and told him her thoughts, but he was back to being grumbly. Now that she knew it was the disease causing the mood swings, she felt more magnanimous about the griping and snippiness.

And less shocked about the crying. She'd never once seen the man get so much as a misty look to his eyes, so seeing him breaking down and sobbing had been jarring, to say the least.

Since Nate was busy filling water bottles, Tammy wandered around the house, looking for a cellar door. There wasn't anything visible, so she went back into the house to talk to the children.

"Hey, Carl?" she called from the foot of the stairs. It was just a moment before the kid popped his head over the banister. His face was blotchy, and Tammy wondered if he'd been crying, possibly due to having to leave the last place he'd felt safe. She swallowed hard.

"Do you know if your GG had a root cellar?" she asked. His frown told her he didn't know what she was talking about. "Like a place that goes underground. A basement, or—"

"Behind the barn," he said, though he shook his head. "We're not 'sposed to go in there though. GG always said there was bad things in it."

That caused Tammy to frown herself. "Oh, okay," she told him as she started to walk away. "Thanks." He nodded and went back to whatever he was doing.

Probably reminiscing. Poor kid.

She went back outside and headed toward the barn. She passed Nate, who seemed bent on ignoring her, but she prayed out loud as she passed. Loud enough for him to hear.

"Okay, Father, we need food, so I'm counting on You to provide for us. Let this cellar be filled with things we can easily carry."

Out of the corner of her eye, she saw Nate glance up, but she continued on her way. It seemed that she aggravated him when he was in the bad mood, so she decided she'd avoid him as much as possible until his mood switched. She wondered if he'd ever have a happy mood with the disease and prayed that it would happen.

As she approached the barn, Tammy thought about what Chrissy had said, that she needed to be praying more. Since the Lord seemed to be answering her prayers, she decided that she would make sure Nate heard them. Well, most of them. The prayers she sent up about keeping her from strangling her husband in his sleep probably didn't need to be shared.

That was one area she felt like she could do better... praying. It seemed she talked to the Lord a lot, but she didn't spend much time listening. *Prayer and meditation,* she told herself. *Especially the meditation.*

The barn looked like it was barely keeping upright—worm eaten boards, peeling paint, and big holes where wood was completely missing. The doors looked like they hadn't been opened in decades, the hinges so rusted they bled copper down the sides. She was glad she didn't have to go into the structure.

Tammy went around to the back and frowned at all the mess. Debris was strewn about—tumbling stacks of lumber, some sort of rusting engine, a golf cart lying on its side and the carcass of an old truck with weeds growing through the body.

Behind some ancient-looking farm equipment that was so weather-worn it looked like it was going to crumble into rusty dust, was a patch of wildflowers. It was so out of place amongst all the rubble that Tammy had a sneaky suspicion it was hiding the door she was looking for. If she hadn't been told where to look, she wouldn't have glanced twice at the area, other than to say, "Oh, pretty flowers."

She had to shove aside an old metal toolbox that

was missing its lid and push a wheelbarrow with a flat tire out of the way just to get to the flower patch. But once she had the area cleared, she pushed through the flowers, sneezing as the pollen dusted her face, and saw what looked like newer wood underneath. If she hadn't known better, she would have thought it was just a piece of plywood lying amongst all the other discarded items. Clearing dirt and dead leaves away, she saw a handle.

And there was a rather old combination lock on a hasp.

Tammy pulled the piece of paper she'd found out of her shorts pocket and entered the numbers in groups of two, leaving off the zero at the end. She was thrilled when it opened after a hard yank.

The hinges creaked like a door in a cheesy haunted house movie, making her giggled nervously. Cobwebs parted as she pushed the door all the way open, and she stared into the entrance. She really, *really* hated spiders. And snakes. And centipedes. Pretty much anything that crawled. She swallowed hard, then squeezed her eyes shut.

Okay, Lord, gonna need Your help. You know how much this is gonna freak me out, so please go before me and clear out anything that might bite. Or sting... or just touch me, cuz yuck!

She almost laughed when a strong breeze came up from behind her and blew the cobwebs out of the way, sticking them to the sides of the beams leading down the stairs. The entryway looked almost clean. She did laugh then.

"Thanks, Dad," she murmured, then sighed. "Don't suppose You'd wanna light the place up, would You?" The stairs stayed dark, though she really was expecting Him to just illuminate the place. He was being so faithful in answering her prayers.

"Darn," she said, sighing with disappointment. "Well, here goes nothing."

Carefully avoiding the cobwebs, she put her hand on one of the beams as she started down the steps. She had only gotten to the third step when her hand bumped something hard. Turning to see an old-fashioned oil lantern, Tammy pulled it off the nail it hung from and stared at it. It almost looked like it had been hung there recently, as it wasn't even dusty. And, thankfully, there weren't any cobwebs.

She stared at the unfamiliar object. It was old, probably older than her mother. She'd seen something like it on television. Thinking back to one particular movie, she turned the thing around, studying it, remembering how the character in the movie lit his lantern like a candle. And the one in her hands did have a sort of wick in the center of it.

Remembering her recent find, she dug her other hand into her shorts pocket and pulled out one of the boxes of matches. She had to hang the lantern back up to light one, then held her breath as she pushed the glass dome up and put the match to the wick. She'd never lit something like that before and she prayed she didn't blow herself up. Of course, she told herself that it was entirely possible the thing didn't even have oil...

It lit immediately.

Tammy laughed as she thanked the Lord again. The light was dim, but there was a little knob on the base, so she turned it, grinning when the light grew brighter.

Holding the lantern up and in front of her, she

proceeded down the rest of the steps, surprised at how deep the cellar was. It had to be a good ten feet underground and she was amazed at how cool it was, almost as if it had central air conditioning.

As she walked forward, she felt even more shock at the sheer size of the cellar. The barn was a huge structure, large enough to be a small aircraft hangar, and it seemed the cellar went under at least half of it. She wondered how in the world people had dug out such a space, and thought maybe they'd dug it first, then built the barn on top. Remembering the falling-down barn, she glanced up and was thankful to see that the cellar roof had been reinforced with wood beams. At least she wouldn't have to worry about a cave in.

Typical of most "tornado alley" cellars, there were a few cots along the wall, the mattresses rolled up and sealed in big garbage bags. That made sense, she thought, since the cellar was damp. Anything cloth would get moldy quickly.

She moved around slowly, looking at everything, trying to determine if there was something they could use for their journey. Boxes labeled "pots and pans," "dishes," and "soap" filled one shelf, while another shelf had Mason jars filled with what looked like nuts, bolts, screws and the like. She thought that was a strange thing to horde in a cellar, but she dismissed it when the lantern's light caught the shelves on the back wall.

It was floor to ceiling, filled with plastic tubs, but it was the labels on the tubs that caught her eye.

"Dairy," said one. "Pork." "Beef." Numerous tubs were labeled with the names of different vegetables.

Tammy moved to the shelves and set her lantern

on the ground, then pulled one of the tubs off. She was disappointed by how little it weighed, obviously being mostly empty. But when she popped open the lid, she let out a squeal of delight.

It was nearly full of freeze-dried packages.

She pulled tub after tub off the shelves, finding all the same thing—they were all filled with packages of freeze-dried food. Lightweight, incredibly long shelf-life, and easy to carry. Even the kids could carry a dozen pounds' worth of food, since it weighed a fraction of that once it was dried.

Tammy left her discovery and went to find Nate. The man apparently had finished filling their water bottles and she went into the house to find him. He was sitting at the dining table, staring out the window. She thought that was odd, but she didn't mention it.

"Hey," she said by way of greeting. He seemed to startle, and he looked at her with wide eyes. She motioned out the window, toward the barn.

"I found a cellar," she told him, "filled with freeze-dried food," she added with a grin. "More than enough for five people for months. The Lord sure answered that prayer."

Instead of having the excitement that she felt, he just nodded. Tammy couldn't help but frown at his lack of reaction, but then wondered if this was just another one of the mood swings—this one "apathy." At least it was better than anger.

The kids must have heard her talking, because they came down the stairs then, carrying their belongings in plastic grocery bags. Tammy smiled at them.

"Do you guys want to see something cool?" she

asked. The girls just stared at her, but Carl nodded a bit reluctantly.

"C'mon," she told them as she started out of the dining room. "You too, honey," she called back to Nate, who seemed to startle out of his thoughts once again. He rose, though, without further prompting.

Tammy led them to the cellar and had to coax the kids to go down the stairs. She'd left the lantern on, hanging from another nail at the bottom of the stairs, so at least it wasn't dark, but the kids seemed afraid of the area for some reason. She asked why.

"GG said it was haunted," Carl told her, his cheeks coloring. "I never believed it though," he quickly added with what Tammy was sure was false bravado.

She smiled at him. "I'm sure you didn't." She stepped down the stairs and pulled the lantern off the nail as she went. When she reached the bottom, she turned and held the lantern up so the others could see.

"I was down here for a little while and didn't see any ghosts," she assured the kids. "Or even any spiders. But I did pray first and ask the Lord to clear it out."

That seemed to reassure the girls, at least, and they moved cautiously down the steps with Carl following and Nate bringing up the rear. She glanced at her husband, relieved to see that he seemed to have come out of his stupor somewhat. And he didn't look angry.

Tammy motioned to the back of the cellar. "Over here," she said with a smile over her shoulder. "Look what the Lord provided for us!" She waved her hand at the tubs on the floor. She'd only pulled down a few and the shelves were still lined with more. It was more than enough food for their trip, she thought.

Nate made a noncommittal grunt which surprised her a bit. Tammy figured it was because she'd given the Lord credit. Of course, her religion-hating husband would find fault with that, she thought with a touch of sorrow. If only he'd realize that it was about having a relationship with the Lord. But, the best she could do was improve her own relationship with Him and continue to pray out loud so that Nate would see how the Lord was answering her prayers.

The kids were a lot more impressed with the find, however, and they dug through the tubs like they were opening Christmas presents. Lou found a package that caused her to gasp—one of only two sounds the girl had made so far. She showed it to Carl, who grinned when he read it.

He glanced up at Tammy. "Salt water taffy," he said with a laugh. "GG always kept bags of it for us." His face fell then, obviously feeling the grief at losing a favored loved one all over again.

"Well, we need to find something that we can use to carry all this food!" Tammy said, keeping her voice overly chipper as she changed the subject. Nate glanced at her with an annoyed look. She gave him a toothy grin in response.

Great. Grumpy Nate is back.

Lou leaned over and whispered something to her brother, who nodded. Tammy was surprised; she'd thought the girls might have been traumatized so much that they were mute, but it seemed it was selective. Carl smiled at his sister and nodded. The girl stood, glanced at Nate and then Tammy, then skirted around them and ran up the cellar stairs.

Tammy looked back at Carl. "Where is she going?"

Carl glanced at the cellar entrance. "To the house. She said there were still some of GG's purses in her closet." He shrugged. "Figured we could use those to carry the food."

Tammy nodded. Handbags weren't going to carry very many food packages. What they needed were more backpacks, or better, duffel bags.

"I'm afraid we're gonna need something bigger than purses," she told Carl. He glanced at the pack of food in his hands, then tilted his head, considering. He nodded.

"Yeah, you're right," he said with a defeated sound.

"Well, Lord," Tammy said with a slight sigh, "You provided the food and blessed us with being able to refill our water bottles, now You need to give us a way to carry all this food. We have a long way to go." She ignored the scowl Nate shot at her and pulled another tub off the shelf, popping the lid.

She laughed immediately, causing Carl, Sissy and Nate to look at her in question. She motioned to the tub. "Look." The kids stood from where they'd been squatting and walked over to her. Carl laughed, and even Sissy made a sound of surprise. Apparently, Nate's curiosity got the better of him, as he, too, walked over to peer in.

The tub contained four duffel bags, and they all had two straps, so they could be slung over the back and worn like a backpack. There was no doubt the Lord Himself had put them there. Tammy said as much.

"Yeah right," Nate snorted, his lip curled up. He glanced at Tammy. "You really think *God* put that there?" he asked sarcastically.

Tammy forced her expression to remain pleasant, but it was very difficult. "Yeah, I do," she said with a nod, waving her hand over the tub. "I'm certain that the *Creator of the entire universe* could provide us with whatever it is we need." She turned her back on him and pulled out a duffel, examining it.

She heard Nate suck in a breath, then turn on his heel and walk to the stairs. Tammy dropped the duffel back in the tub as she frowned after him, watching as he stomped up the steps.

"What's wrong with him?" Carl asked. Tammy shrugged as she glanced down at the boy.

"He, uh, he's having a hard time believing in Jesus," she said, putting her hands up in a helpless gesture.

Carl nodded with a sage look that made Tammy want to chuckle. "Dad was the same way," he said. "Mom too, but she got saved and baptized," he said with a grin. "Couple months after, Dad gave in." His grin faded as another sad look crossed his face.

"Wasn't much later that they were in a car accident."

Tammy made a noise of distress and put her arm around the boy's shoulders. He stiffened at first, but then relaxed into her. "I'm sorry, sweetie," she said, then held out a hand to Sissy. She didn't expect the girl to take it, but was surprised when she reached for it, curling her small fingers around Tammy's.

"At least you know that they're with the Lord in Heaven now," she said with a smile. She knew it wasn't much to comfort children who might not really understand the concept, but it was all she could say.

Carl nodded. "Yeah. Guess it's kinda a good thing

they're not here now. Now with... stuff the way it is." A shrug lifted his narrow shoulders. Tammy gave him a soft squeeze.

"That's true," she said, surprised at the young boy's insight. "Sometimes I think it would be nice if we weren't here either."

Carl tilted his head. "When do you think the, uh, the... what's it called? When Jesus takes us off the ground."

Tammy smiled. "Teachers have called it the rapture," she said.

He nodded. "Yeah, that. Shouldn't it have happened already?"

She shook her head. "No, I don't think so. Not anymore, anyway. I always thought it was gonna happen before all the trouble started, but now I think it's not happening until... uh, the very end."

Tammy wasn't sure how much Carl had been taught about the Tribulation Period and she really didn't want to share what she knew. If they weren't going to be "taken off the ground" any time soon, she knew they were facing some really difficult times.

But the Lord will be faithful. He always was. It was believers who faltered, who feared and worried and stumbled when things didn't turn out the way they'd thought they would or should.

It made her wonder how many had fallen away from their beliefs already, since the rapture hadn't happened yet. Most of those she'd known had. It made her heart ache to think about and said a quick prayer that they'd return to the Lord... and especially that they wouldn't take the mark of the beast when the time came for that decision.

Lou came back down the steps then, carrying three handbags. Carl smiled at his sister, then motioned to the tub. "Look what God gave us," he said as she stepped closer. "Since there's only four big bags, I think God wanted Sissy to carry one of them purses." He pulled out a duffel. "You and me can carry one of these, cuz we're bigger."

Tammy looked at Carl and Lou with a critical eye. They were so thin, she thought one of the bags would pull them right over. She decided to make sure the kids carried the lightest of the packages.

They were busy sorting the foil packs when Nate finally reappeared. He walked down the steps slowly, eyeing them as he approached. Tammy lifted an eyebrow in question, hoping that grouchy Nate was gone. Of course, sad Nate wasn't any easier to deal with.

"Uh, need some help?" he asked as he squatted next to the tub Carl was sitting beside. The boy grinned at him.

"Yeah, you can help fill the duffel bags Jesus gave us," he said, turning to give Tammy a cheeky wink. She snorted out a laugh, then cleared her throat to cover it.

"Oh, look," she said as a distraction from Nate's suspicious look toward her, "Lima beans. My favorite!" They weren't, not by a long shot. Nate knew that too, and he frowned at her, then shook his head and chuckled.

Tammy grinned. *Oh good! Happy Nate finally showed up!*

They all worked together, chatting about nothing important, when Sissy suddenly fell over onto her side, eyes closed. Tammy let out a gasp as she scrambled up to get to her. Carl's laugh stopped her.

"She does that when she gets tired," he said, shaking his head with a grin. "Just falls over, asleep." Another sad look crossed his face then.

"Used to freak Mom out too."

Sissy couldn't have been more than five, Tammy thought, and she wondered how old she'd been when her parents had died. She decided she'd ask Carl about it when the girls weren't around. Every time he mentioned their parents, Lou got such a devastated look that it literally hurt Tammy's chest to see it.

"Well, maybe we ought to take her into the house and put her in the bed," Tammy suggested. She'd been surprised to hear that the kids had been sharing that tiny daybed, but since it was the only thing with a mattress in the house, it made sense. It must have been as crowded for them as the little bed in Gerald's cellar had been for her and Nate.

Carl was protective of his sisters, though, so it was no surprise that he would have made sure he was with them at all times. Tammy thought the protectiveness was a good thing, though she hated the idea of why he'd come to be that way.

Shaking off her dreary thoughts, she pulled out another package of freeze-dried cheese and shoved it into Sissy's purse. The thing was already full, and she lifted it, thankful that it hardly weighed anything. She'd picked the only purse that was fabric and not imitation leather, as it was the most lightweight. It wouldn't be waterproof in the least, but since the food was all pack in foil-type envelopes, it wouldn't matter.

Once the older kids had duffel bags full of vegetables—which were also not too heavy—she and Nate loaded two more with the meats.

"Save some room for water bottles in one of them," Nate told her as he stood. "I'll take Sissy to her room and get the backpacks."

Tammy winced but nodded. That was going to make for a very heavy bag, and she hated that her husband was going to have to carry it.

"God gave the Egyptians water out of a rock when they were in the desert," Carl said after Nate left, carrying the still-sleeping little girl. She hadn't even stirred when he picked her up. "Maybe we don't have to carry so much."

Tammy smiled at him. "They were actually Hebrews escaping Egypt," she gently corrected. He shrugged.

"Don't matter. Still, water outta a rock is pretty cool."

She nodded. "Yeah, it is." She gnawed at her lip as she waited for Nate to come back. Thoughts ran through her mind... of trusting, of believing the Lord would provide, of expecting a miracle.

But then she also thought about scripture that said not to tempt the Lord. And how He had warned Joseph of the coming famine and told him to prepare. She knew there were other stories like that as well, where people were warned to be ready for coming disasters. But there were also plenty of scriptures that said to rely on God for all their needs.

If they didn't have to carry all those water bottles, then he could carry more food. And it wouldn't be such a burden for him either. Her husband still had deep grooves in his shoulders just from the week he'd been hauling water across the state like a pack mule.

Nate came back down the stairs then with the

backpacks. Tammy sucked in a deep breath. *Lord, I know You won't let me down. Please show my husband a true miracle. One he can't deny... so that he can't deny You any longer.*

Nate knelt next to the duffel bag she'd left space in and unzipped his backpack to pull the water bottles out. She put her hand on his arm.

"Wait, honey," she said as she slid her hand down to his hand, then stuck out her other hand to Carl, wiggling her fingers. He frowned in confusion, but he took it.

"Get Lou's hand, and Lou, you hold Nate's other hand." The girl got wide eyes and turned to her brother, who nodded.

"It's okay," he said softly. "Nate won't hurt you." He shot a glare at Nate then, as if to say, "You better not." Nate watched as her husband's lips twitched, but he nodded encouragingly at the little girl, who tentatively reached out and put her hand in his. Nate didn't close his hand, Tammy noticed, probably because he didn't want Lou to think she was trapped.

He's such a good man. At least he was when he wasn't having the anger mood swings.

"We're gonna pray," she said. Out of the corner of her eye she saw Nate stiffen, but she started praying before he could say anything.

"Lord, You've provided so much for us thus far," she said, "and we thank You for all You've done. This food is so wonderful, and we know that You led GG to stock her cellar because You knew that we'd be here this day, needing it. And You provided the means to carry that food, so we thank You for that too.

"But now we're asking You to provide the water we

need for our journey so that Nate doesn't have to lug around all that weight. It's a burden, Father, and one that we know isn't necessary, because You will provide for all the needs of Your children. You are the Creator, after all, and we know that You can make water come from a rock, if You wish. You have before," she added with a laugh.

"So, we're gonna trust You and only take one water bottle each, knowing You'll provide what we need." Nate sucked in a breath at that and squeezed her hand rather hard.

"Yeah, Jesus," Carl added. "We know You'll take care of us, cuz You said You would. You made the water anyway, so it ain't no big deal for You to give us some when we need it."

"Amen," Lou whispered, startling Tammy. Nate, too, jerked slightly.

"Amen!" Tammy said with a grin. She looked at the kids, winking, then turned to Nate.

"Well, that should relieve your burden quite a bit!" she said cheerfully. He narrowed his eyes at her, but she just continued smiling.

"'Trust in the Lord with all your heart and do not lean on your own understanding. In all your ways acknowledge Him, and He will make your paths straight.'"

Tammy whipped her head to Carl, shocked to hear the child quoting from Proverbs. He grinned at her, shrugging.

"GG made us memorize a Bible verse every week. Had to, if we wanted any taffy."

Tammy laughed. "I think your GG was a very smart woman. When I get to Heaven, I'm giving her a big ol' hug."

Carl smiled softly. "Me too," he whispered.

Chapter 8

NATHAN ARGUED against leaving the water bottles behind. It was insanity and he couldn't believe that Tammy would be so naive and stupid to think they could travel with one bottle each. He made his stand clear, but she and the kids pretty much ignored him.

Shockingly, it was Lou who convinced him to give up his fight.

"Jesus is gonna give us water," she whispered as she put her small hand on Nathan's shoulder. She'd stood up when he started telling his wife she was insane, and he'd thought he'd frightened the little girl.

There was a pleading look on her face, along with something that said she trusted what Tammy had said, that the "Lord would provide." Nathan thought it was rubbish, but he wasn't going to be the one to destroy a child's faith. Especially not one so delicate as the little girl who'd obviously been abused.

A heavy sigh left him, and he cocked his neck from side to side to crack it, then smiled at Lou. "Okay," he said, darting a glance at Tammy, who managed to keep a neutral look on her face. He silently dared her to cheer, or even crack a smile, but to her credit, she didn't.

They went back into the house and the kids went upstairs to see if they could manage to take a nap with Sissy, while Nathan and Tammy went into the living room. There was a ratty-looking chair in one corner and a small loveseat that looked like gallons of fruit juice had been spilled on it over the years. Apparently, the neighbors didn't think the furniture was good enough to steal.

"I'll take the chair," Tammy said as she moved over to it, then dragged it closer to the fireplace. Nathan wondered why she would do that, since it was far too hot in the house to need a fire, but then she sat and propped her feet up on the hearth.

"Okay," he said as he settled on the loveseat, "but we'll switch after an hour or so. That way we can both stretch out for a little while at least." She didn't reply and Nathan looked at her, smiling when he saw that she was already asleep. It didn't take long for him to follow.

NATHAN WAS awakened by someone patting his face. He frowned, batting away the offensive intrusion. He felt like he'd just gotten to sleep and needed at least two days more.

"Mister man," a little voice whispered. "Mister man. Wake up! You gots to hurry. Please, Mister man..."

Nathan forced his eyes to open and turned to see Lou standing next to him, a worried look on her face. He blinked a few times, then sat up, rubbing his face. After yawning, he looked back at her. The girl was dancing back and forth from foot to foot.

"What's the matter, honey?" he asked, careful to keep his voice low and soothing. The child startled worse than a yearling doe.

Her eyes darted toward the window. Nathan glanced over to see the barn in the distance. She looked back at him.

"Um, we sorta locked Sissy in the cellar."

"Huh?" Nathan was completely awake at her

admission. "What do you mean?"

The girl's cheeks colored, and she stared at the floor near her feet. "Carl and me went back to the cellar to see if there was more candy," she said in a near whisper. "We gots some more bags and then we was gonna go back to the house and Carl said we had to lock the door, 'case them bad people wanna come steal GG's food." Her voice cracked a little and Nathan told himself to be patient, to wait for her to get the story out in her time.

"Carl put the lock back on and then we heard Sissy crying. Guess she woke up from her nap and snuck down there. We didn't see her!" she wailed.

Nathan put his hand out, careful to be gentle as he awkwardly patted the girl's shoulder. Comforting a child was out of his realm of expertise and he looked over at Tammy, but the woman was still out. She'd always been a heavy sleeper and he knew she was as tired as he was after walking throughout the night and then being up for most of the day.

"Okay, okay, don't cry," he told the girl. "We'll see what we can do to get her out. Don't worry. It's okay."

He stood then and stretched, trying to work the kinks out of his spine. The loveseat had been far too short for his frame, but at least it was better than sleeping in the chair. He walked over and jostled Tammy.

"Tammy, wake up," he said as he lightly shook her by the shoulder. She moaned but didn't open her eyes.

"Honey, you need to wake up," he continued as he shook her a bit harder. That time, she shifted, curling up in the chair like a child.

"She sleeps like Sissy," Lou said. Nathan glanced

at her, giving her a small smile.

"Yeah, she's really tired." *So am I,* he thought, but the kids needed help, so sleep would have to come later. He glanced at the window again, realizing that the sun was low on the horizon. *Well, later tomorrow I guess,* he thought with a sigh.

It took a firmer shake, to the point he nearly jerked her out of the chair before she finally woke up. "Wha... whazz wrong?" she slurred, looking around in confusion. Her eyes focused on Lou, and she frowned.

"What's wrong, sweetie?"

The girl immediately started crying again, blubbering her story. Nathan had to translate and once he did, Tammy was on her feet and out the door.

They ran to the barn and saw Carl with a piece of metal, trying to pry the lock off the chain on the door of the cellar. He looked their way and Nathan frowned at the panicked expression on his face.

"Hey, it's okay," he told the kid as he approached, taking the bar out of his hands before he hurt himself. "We'll get her out. It's okay."

"No, you don't understand!" he shouted. "I... I left the lantern on," he admitted with a sob. "I forgot about it and I think Sissy dropped it. The cellar might be on fire!"

That made Nathan's heart lurch, but he shook his head. "No, lanterns have safety features. It can't just—"

"It's one of those old ones," Tammy reminded him, a stricken look on her face. "Before they had regulations. Like fifties style."

Nathan cursed with such a foul word that Tammy

pursed her lips. He ignored her look and he leaned over to grab the padlock, yanking on it as hard as he could, but it was solid. He straightened to see Tammy digging in her pockets, growing more frantic as she checked and rechecked them.

"I had the combination for the lock!" she cried. "And now it's not here! I don't remember any of the numbers!"

"Go back to the house and look around the chair!" he yelled. Tammy spun on her heel and sprinted in the direction of the house while he took the bar that Carl had been using and tried prying the lock himself. It wouldn't budge.

The chain securing the door was huge, the type they used to tow semitrucks or airplanes. The lock, as well, was old, but very sturdy. He doubted even bolt cutters would get through it, but it was worth a try.

"Are there any tools around here?" he asked Carl. The kid had tears streaming down his face, leaving clean tracks in the dirt. He shook his head.

"Think the neighbors got 'em all."

Nathan cursed again. "How about something I can use to smash the lock?" He gave up trying to pry the lock off and instead moved to the side of the door to try to pry it up from the hinges. Of course, the thing was built with the hinges on the inside, but he hoped he could splinter the wood enough to get it open.

Carl ran around the area, digging in the weeds, looking for something they could use. Nathan's throat worked when he heard Sissy's frightened cries, muffled through the door.

"It's okay, honey!" he called out. "The floor is dirt and that won't catch on fire. It'll be okay!" He felt like a horrible liar, since the shelves were all made of wood, as well as the beams going across the roof. If those caught on fire, there was a very good chance the whole cellar would cave in, burying the little girl.

Tammy came flying around the house then. "I can't find it!" she cried. "What are we gonna do?"

Nathan yelled in frustration and threw the bar away. It clanged against the side of the barn and nearly hit Carl, who looked up, a fearful look on his face. Nathan shook his head.

"Sorry," he muttered then turned to Tammy. "There's no way to get the door open without opening the lock." He hated admitting defeat, but there wasn't anything he could do...

"Wait," he said, then winced as he ran a hand over the back of his neck. It was a nervous habit, he knew, a tell-tale sign that he was feeling out of sorts. He'd been doing it a lot lately. "It's a crazy idea," he admitted, "but at this point, it's all I've got."

"What?" Tammy said, frustration in her voice.

He stared down at the wood door. It was barely more than a piece of plywood and there wasn't any reason why it should be so difficult to get through. He looked back at Tammy.

"We could burn the door."

Her eyes widened and she turned back to stare at the wood, then shook her head. "I guess you didn't notice that it's only wood on the outside," she said, looking back at him. "The inside is sheet metal."

Nathan groaned. "Guess that's why I couldn't pry it off," he sighed. Carl came running up to them then.

"I can't find anything," he said, "'cept an old

toolbox, but I don't think it's heavy enough to break the lock."

Tammy cleared her throat then, a choking sound. She reached out and grabbed Lou's hand, then Carl's. "Grab his hand, honey," she told Nathan. "We're gonna pray the Lord opens this lock for us."

Nathan couldn't help but flick his eyes skyward. They were wasting precious time, time he didn't think Sissy had. If those beams caught fire...

Tammy gave up waiting on him and started praying. "Lord, we need Your help! Please open this lock so we can get to Sissy. And keep her safe until we do. Don't let her be afraid. Hurry, Father!"

Nathan turned and started to run off to the house, determined to find something he could use to smash that lock open, though he was afraid it was going to take a sledgehammer that he was sure wasn't available. He made a mental note to stop on their journey and punch out the thieving neighbors.

He'd just gotten a dozen yards away when he heard excited exclamations and glanced over his shoulder. What he saw stopped him so suddenly, he almost fell over. He stared back at the sight of his wife and the kids.

And the open cellar door.

His feet felt like he was wearing cement shoes as he walked back to them. Tammy was already down the stairs and Nathan noticed tendrils of smoke drifting up through the door. It wasn't a lot of smoke, thankfully.

Carl and Lou were bobbing up and down next to the door and he knew that Tammy had told them to wait for her. It was just moments before his wife appeared with a huge grin on her face... and a thumb-sucking Sissy in her arms.

"She's just fine!" she called out as they ascended the stairs. "Just like Shadrach, Meshach and Abednego, she doesn't even smell like smoke!" she laughed as she set the girl down.

Nathan had a flicker of memory at those names, knowing he'd heard them before, but he couldn't quite put his finger on it. Something he'd heard as a child, he thought. Maybe he'd ask Tammy about it later.

Whatever it was, Carl knew, because he laughed. "That's cuz Jesus was in the fire with her!"

That comment made Nathan grit his teeth. *Not that again...*

His eyes were drawn to the open cellar door then. He could see the metal Tammy had mentioned. It was thick and was attached to the hinges on the inside of the frame. The wood was just a covering, he realized. There would have been no way he could have pried that thing up. It would have taken a cutting torch or a plasma cutter.

The chain was still looped through the handle, and he stared at it for a moment. The links were as thick as his forefinger, and each ring was as long as his hand. Again, no way to get through it without power tools or incendiary heat.

He looked down to see the lock in the weeds. There was no way it could have been broken into, he realized, probably not even with a sledgehammer. It was massive, as big as his fist, likely made of hardened steel. Something created to make sure it couldn't be cut. Or smashed. Yet, it was open.

Nathan couldn't explain it.

"Some things are unexplainable except by God's

hand..."

The voice in his head made him startle and he looked, wondering who'd spoken. But it was a male voice, a rather deep one. There was no way it could have been Tammy or Carl.

"Great, more craziness from the CJD," he muttered to himself. The others didn't hear him, as they were busy fussing over Sissy. The little girl was smiling around her thumb, seemingly unshaken by her experience.

Carl asked her if she was okay as he patted her down, like he was feeling for injuries. She pulled her thumb out of her mouth then and grinned at her brother.

"Jesus was with me," she said. It was the first time Nathan had heard her speak. Judging by the twin looks on her siblings' faces, it apparently was an anomaly.

Carl laughed as he hugged her. "That's what I thought. 'Member GG always said Jesus protects us when we ask."

The thumb went back into Sissy's mouth and Nathan wondered if she was thinking the same thing he was—if "Jesus" protected people, why wasn't He there when the kids were getting abused? Why wasn't He there when Tammy was suffering so much at the hands of her self-righteous evil-minded father?

Because He doesn't exist, he told himself with gritted teeth.

After making sure the fire was out—which had burned two full shelves and melted several empty tubs—they secured the cellar door once more and went to the water pump to get some "washing up water" at

Tammy's insistence.

"We might not be able to take baths or showers right now," she told the grumbling kids as she made them scrub their faces, hands and arms, "but we can at least try to be as clean as possible. Cleanliness is next to godliness!"

Carl rolled his eyes at her. "That ain't in the Bible."

Tammy grinned at him. "I know it isn't, but it's a good principle. Remember that even Jesus washed His disciples' feet."

Sissy stuck her foot out. "Wash mine," she told Carl, making them all laugh.

AFTER THE near disaster in the cellar, Sissy came out of her mute shell and talked non-stop. Nathan was almost wishing the little girl would go back to her silent state when she started asking ridiculous questions as they plodded along across fields and pastures.

"How come I can't see my eyes?"

"You can," Tammy told the little girl. "You just have to look in the mirror."

"Why do dogs gots tails, but people don't gots them?"

"Cuz we're not animals, silly," Lou told her sister. Nathan kept his mouth shut, reserving judgment on that.

"How come the stars don't fall down?"

Nathan started to answer that one with an explanation of space and gravity that would have been over her head and would hopefully shut her up for a bit, but Carl beat him to it.

"Cuz God keeps them in the sky where He wants them."

Nathan's jaw was starting to ache.

He thought traveling with Tammy was an exercise in patience with her need for frequent stops, but the kids—especially the girls—made their journey move along at a snail's pace. In the winter. Through frozen mud. On a bicycle. With flat tires.

Nathan's patience was nearing the end when Lou said she needed to "potty."

"You just went half an hour ago!" he snapped at her. Ten hours before, his tone would have made the girl shrink away, but now she just shrugged.

"Gotta go," she said simply.

Tammy chuckled and she dropped her duffel bag next to Nathan, while the others did the same. "C'mon, honey," she said to Lou as she held out her hand. She was already holding Sissy's hand, so she led the two little girls off into a thicket.

Carl watched them and called out, "Watch for sna—"

"Shh!" Nathan said as he clapped his hand over the kid's mouth. Carl looked up at him with wide eyes.

"Do not mention snakes," Nathan murmured as he released the kid's mouth. "Or spiders. Or any bugs, really." He shook his head. "Girls are kinda... weird about those things. Just let them pee and hope nothing is out there."

Carl grinned at him, the moonlight catching his teeth, making them shine. Nathan looked up at the sky, at the waning moon. He wished he had some sort of an idea which stars were which and where they should be at certain times of the year. He could only guesstimate it was August, but he really had no idea what the day was. When everything fell apart, it didn't seem to matter much any longer.

It was funny, the things they used to think were so important. Like getting tickets to the Indy races every year. Hoping the Hoosiers beat Purdue. Worrying over taxes and high utility bills. Wanting to get a bigger, better, newer... whatever.

Now they were happy to make it through another day.

Nathan supposed "happy" wasn't the right word. There wasn't anything pleasing about their life now, not by a longshot. He couldn't even say they were content. There was never enough rest to be had, or enough safety. He couldn't remember the last time he'd been able to fully relax. And until they got to Gerald's, they hadn't had enough food. At least they had enough now, thanks to the stash at the farmhouse.

But they sure didn't have enough water.

He was still angry about that, about letting Tammy and the kids bully him into not bringing the water bottles. He was blaming the CJD for making him so soft; otherwise, he would have told them all to shove their stupid religious beliefs where the sun didn't shine and packed the bottles.

Nathan shrugged his shoulders then, huffing out a small laugh when he realized his back and neck seemed to be thankful for the lighter load.

The girls took long enough that Nathan was about to go after them, but they finally reappeared from out of the thicket. Strangely, Sissy was in the lead with

Lou and Tammy following. So far, the youngest never ventured away from her siblings or Tammy, but she was a good couple of yards ahead of them. When he realized why, he thought his heart was going to seize.

A man had Tammy by the throat.

He was behind Tammy with his arm wrapped around her front. Even in the pale light, Nathan could tell by the way his wife was walking that the man had something pressed against her back, some sort of weapon.

As they drew closer, Sissy bolted for Carl, who wrapped his arm around her, tucking her into his side. Lou started to run ahead as well, but the man growled for her to stop. The girl immediately obeyed, which was strange for a six-year-old. Nathan wondered again just what the girl had gone through, what kind of punishment she'd suffered for not being obedient in the past.

The man jerked on Tammy, pulling her to a stop. "Put your hands up," he told Nathan. He did so, slowly.

"It's okay, man," Nathan told him in a soothing voice. "We're not gonna do anything. Just let her go." He called on the negotiator training he'd had with the police department in "talking down" suiciders and terrorists. *Keep your voice steady and soft. Be friendly. Try to soothe them...*

"Don't move," the guy growled, though Nathan hadn't taken a step. He glanced down at Carl, noticing the kid had moved closer to him, close enough that he was against his side.

"We're good," Nathan told him. "No one's gonna do anything," he repeated. He noticed the guy wasn't wearing a Neos uniform, at least, but he seemed as crazy as those belonging to that group did.

Maybe even more so.

"Daddy, I'm scared," Carl whimpered as he snuggled even closer. That caught Nathan off-guard, and he stiffened for a second, wondering if the trauma of the situation had triggered something in the kid. But then he felt Carl's hand slide up under his shirt, to the waistband.

Where his gun was.

Nathan wasn't sure how he felt about the kid reaching for his weapon, but truthfully, he had nothing to offer himself, other than trying to keep a desperate, crazy person from losing his cool completely with just his voice.

"It's okay... son," Nathan said awkwardly. He glanced down at Carl, impressed to see the kid acting like he was terrified. Of course, he told himself, the kid probably *was* terrified that his sisters were going to be hurt, or worse. He was probably worried about Tammy as well. The kids all seemed to have taken to her.

He looked back at the man, his eyes flickering over Tammy. He was surprised to see that she didn't look as frightened as even Carl did; in fact, his wife looked downright angry. Her eyes flashed in the moonlight and Nathan knew what she was saying—*Take this guy out, now!*

But he couldn't make a move without risking her getting hurt. Whatever the man was holding at her back was most likely sharp, since Tammy had her back arched quite a bit, as if trying not to be impaled.

Carl slid the gun up a little bit, but it got caught on the fabric. The kid tugged a little harder and Nathan was thankful it wasn't a revolver; otherwise, he might have been missing a chunk out of his backside.

The kid slid the gun free just as the man said, "I want all them packs you got there." He nodded toward the duffel bags behind them. "Hand 'em over and I might let you live." He grinned then, and even in the pale light, Nathan could see the man had a severe lack of dental hygiene.

"All right," Nathan said. "Just don't hurt the girls, okay? Just let us go on our way—"

"Shut up!" the man said. "I give the orders."

Nathan didn't speak then, not wanting to aggravate the man, but he nodded. Carl whimpered as he moved behind him, then sobbed loudly to cover the distinctive click of a round being chambered in the nine-millimeter.

The man started to speak, but Nathan spoke up first. "The boy is... uh, special," he said. "He doesn't understand."

The man sneered at that, but he just jerked his head toward the duffels. "Get 'em and bring 'em over here," he instructed. Nathan nodded, but before he could move, he heard Carl murmuring.

"Please Lord, let my aim be as good as David's. I need to hit this Goliath in the forehead too."

When Nathan realized what the kid meant, he turned to tell him "No!" because the last thing he wanted was some kid shooting a gun anywhere near Tammy. But before he could say anything, Carl stepped out from behind him and pulled the trigger.

The man fell flat on his back, a bullet wound in the middle of his forehead.

The girls burst into tears and Tammy hugged them

to her, shielding them from the sight of the dead man. Carl rushed forward to comfort his sisters as well, but Nathan had the presence of mind to snatch the gun out of his hand. Carl grinned back at him.

"Almost forgot about that."

Nathan scowled at him, then looked at weapon. His eyes widened as he saw that the safety was still on. He doubted Carl'd had the presence of mind to engage it, since he'd admitted he'd forgotten about having the gun.

He shook his head, wondering how the weapon had fired, but his wife stepped toward him since Carl had his sisters in a hug, so he tucked the gun back into his waistband, then reached out for her. She still looked angry, though relieved. He held her close, shaking from the fear—and the feeling of helplessness.

After a long while, Nathan turned, tucking Tammy into his side, his arm slung protectively over her shoulders. He wasn't sure his heart was going to beat normally for a long time. A very long time.

"Where in the world'd you learn to shoot like that?" he asked Carl, who had both sisters clinging to him. The boy grinned.

"Movies. Video games. That was the first time I ever shot a real gun though," he admitted.

Nathan felt his mouth drop open; that shot would have been impressive for the best of marksmen. He doubted he himself would have been that accurate. It was mostly dark, for one thing, and for another—three inches to the right would have made the difference in killing the assailant... or hitting Tammy.

And that thought angered him, greatly.

"Then why in the h—" Tammy elbowed him in the

ribs, and he paused to suck in a breath. He'd been about to go off on the kid who had likely just saved all their lives.

He let the breath out in a slow sigh. "Why did you take the risk of hitting Tammy then?" He thought he'd managed to keep his tone calm, but Tammy nudged him again.

Carl shrugged. "I knew the Lord would do the aiming," he said simply. "I just had to be willing to pull the trigger."

Nathan frowned at that, but he didn't say anything. Tammy, however, spoke up.

"Well, thank you for being so faithful, sweetie." She stepped away from Nathan then, and he had to fight back the urge to yank her back to him. She wrapped her arms around the three children, who all seemed to soak in the attention.

Nathan realized with a pang that Tammy would have been a good mother. She was kind and considerate, putting their needs before her own. And she'd shown immense patience when she'd sat and brushed the girls' matted hair, which had taken hours of gentle tugging and coaxing. He would have just hacked it all off and been done with it.

They'd decided early in their marriage to get financially stable before starting a family. They both wanted good jobs with steady income and benefits, to save enough money for a down payment on a house, and to pay off their cars. All those plans had fallen apart one after another as real life took over and so did the family planning.

Now he was glad it had. The crazy world they found themselves in was no place to raise a family. It was a shame the kids now in their care were likely going to have to suffer through even worse than what they had that night.

Nathan started worrying about Carl, about how he would react once the realization hit him that he had killed a man. Nathan himself had never been in that situation, though he knew a few fellow officers who had. One of them ended up quitting the force over it.

"Are you okay?" Tammy asked the kid, as if mirroring his thoughts. "I mean—" she turned and glanced down at the man and the dark puddle forming under his head in the parched earth.

She turned back to Carl. "You killed a man," she said gently. "It's okay," she quickly added. "He was going to hurt—"

"Nah, it's fine," Carl said with another nonchalant shrug. "When he first walked out with you, I started prayin'. God told me he was a bad guy and not one of His kids, that he wasn't gonna 'cept Him, ever. It was okay to kill him."

Tammy laughed and hugged the kid closer while Nathan rolled his eyes. *Great, now I have another religious nut to deal with.*

The rest of the evening went much better after that, since the girls seemed more reluctant to ask for "potty breaks." Of course, the lessening breaks were also due to having to conserve their water, since they only had one bottle each, he thought with gritted teeth. *Stupid.*

When the girls started dance-walking, though, Tammy insisted on taking them behind a bush, while Nathan demanded she take the smaller handgun with her.

Of course, the stubborn woman protested, saying

she had her crossbow. "You can't keep an arrow nocked in it," he told her, frustration in his tone, "and that isn't a close-range weapon. Just take the blasted gun, for crying out loud!" Thankfully, she'd listened and even decided afterward to keep it in her pocket.

When the sun started glowing on the horizon, they moved into a thick grove of trees and set up the tent they'd found amongst the camping supplies. They ate their only meal of the day—though Tammy insisted the kids eat frequent snacks to keep up their strength as they walked—and then the girls curled into each other, with Tammy in the middle. All three were softly snoring within moments.

Carl sat next to Nathan, who was propped against two stacked duffels, watching the girls. "Wish I could sleep like that," the kid murmured. Nathan looked at him in question.

"You have insomnia too?"

Carl nodded. "Yeah, ever since... well, since foster care," he said with bitterness. Nathan held out the packet of candy that had come in his freeze-dried meal and Carl took one, popping it in his mouth. Nathan picked up his water bottle to take a small sip and frowned; the bottle was nearly full, and he'd been sipping from it all night.

Huh. Guess I wasn't drinking as much as I thought.

"I had to watch out for them," Carl said as he chewed. "'Specially Lou. Mister Walters had a... thing for little girls," he sneered. "Pig."

Nathan nodded with his own sneer. "Agreed. Too bad we can't go back and kick some Walters butt, eh?"

That caused Carl to laugh. "Yeah, that would be nice," he nodded. "I wasn't too good at fighting him off." He pulled his dishwater blonde hair off his forehead then, pointing. Nathan had to lean closer and squint to see what he was pointing at. It was a jagged scar that ran across his hairline.

"That's from a dresser drawer," he said. "Mister Walters yanked it out of the dresser and hit me with it when I jumped him from behind. He was gonna..." His face took on a haunted look. He glanced back at Nathan.

"He was in the girls' room. Getting into Lou's bed."

Nathan's back teeth felt like they were going to crack from the pressure he was exerting on them to keep from saying what he really wanted to say.

"Well, glad you were there to help the girls," he managed to grit out.

Carl shook his head. "Not always," he said sadly.

Nathan patted the kid on the knee. "You did all you could, little man. And that—that Walters guy—" what he really wanted to call the guy wasn't fit for a kids' ears, "—will get what's coming to him in the end."

Carl's mouth scrunched to the side. "I hope not," he said. It shocked Nathan.

"Why the hel—why not?" He was starting to think the kid *was* special.

Carl shrugged again in that careless way only a young teen could. "Don't want no one going to Hell," he said as his eyes turned to his sisters again. "I wouldn't wish that on my worst enemy." He glanced back at Nathan.

"God wants everyone to come to Him," he continued, "even the bad guys. Don't matter what they did, neither. If they 'cept Jesus, then they get to go to

Heaven."

"But... but that's..." Nathan didn't even know how to respond to such a ridiculous statement. Carl laughed.

"I know, sounds crazy. But that's just how God is. He loves everyone that much. He died for us, you know. For me, for my sisters, for Tammy, for Mister Walters, for that guy back in the field with the bullet hole in his head."

He turned and stared intently at Nathan. "And for you, too, Nathan. He died for you and He's just waiting for you to give your live to Him."

Nathan couldn't help the snort and was sure the smile that crossed his face was more of a sneer. "And how would you know that, little man?"

It was ludicrous to think that "God"—if He existed—would want criminals, child molesters, and yeah, even a misguided Jew who denied Him all his life, to be in Heaven with Him.

"I know that," Carl said, "cuz Jesus told me so."

Chapter 9

H E'S NEVER *going to accept the Lord. There isn't any hope. And the time is short.*

"Why do you think that?"

I turn, trying to see who is talking, but the mist surrounding me is too thick. It reminds me of the fog I got lost in when my parents took me to San Francisco as a child. I'd wandered just a little too far from Mother... and then I couldn't find her. I panicked, crying out, begging her to find me.

Father found me instead.

My mind reels at the memory, of the beating I'd suffered that early morning. I'd had to go to the Sunday School class at the church we were visiting with a bloody nose and a backside so sore I refused to sit.

I was certain the teacher didn't believe my go-to story of tripping and falling. But she didn't say anything. Didn't do anything.

No one ever did.

There's a light in this mist. I'm sure that's where the voice came from, and I take a step toward it. But something—or someone—is holding me back, not wanting me to go to the light that beckons me, like a warm fire on a cold winter's night. There's love in that light. And healing. Forgiveness.

But the mist doesn't want me to find it.

"Who are you?" I call out, but I'm not given an answer. Instead, the mist swirls around me, slithering around my legs, wispy tendrils snaking up my sides. I bat at it, but it has no substance, though I know it

wants to hold me back.

"I Am," the voice says simply.

I frown, but I don't ask for clarity. I pull my leg forward again, but if feels as if I've stepped into thick, half-frozen mud. I silently beg my feet to move as the mist rises up my body, I find it's harder to breathe.

"Don't give up," the voice continues. "Keep praying. Nathan will come to Me..."

"Lord?" I call out, my chest aching with the need to get to Him. My heart is the only thing capable of moving now, as the mist has completely surrounded me in a cloying cocoon.

Keep praying," He says again. I know that voice... it's my Shepherd! I struggle further, trying to escape the mist as the dark tendrils encompass my body like slithering snakes. It feels... evil. It doesn't want me getting near the Lord. It wants me to stay where I am, immobile. Incapable. Incapacitated.

Useless.

"Keep praying. If you ask, I will hear and answer..." the voice has faded to little more than a whisper and my throat constricts with emotion. I don't want Him to leave! I need Him here, with me, to help me. I open my mouth to call out, but no sound escapes me. The tendrils have choked out the last of my breath.

I'm going to die here...

TAMMY'S EYES shot open as she sucked in a gasp of air while looking around frantically. It took a moment to realize that she was in a tent... and surrounded by little arms and legs.

No wonder I thought I was being suffocated, she

laughed to herself as she carefully pulled Sissy's arm off her neck, placing it on the child's side. Lou was on her other side, her arm across Tammy's chest and a leg over her thighs. Tammy realized then she wasn't going to be able to extricate herself without waking the girls up, so she resigned herself to staying put.

The walls of the tent were glowing faintly, and she knew that it must be nearing dusk, signaling the need to prepare for another long night's walk. She sighed; she was so tired of walking and knew that they still had a very long way to go.

Nate had said they were in Kentucky. That had been a huge disappointment to her; not that she didn't like the state, but she'd hoped they'd be further along. When she'd asked her husband how long it would take them to get to wherever it was they were supposed to be going, he had hedged, obviously not wanting to share that information. All he'd said was he wanted to make sure they were out of the Midwest before Autumn, before the snow came.

Tammy thought that was a stellar idea, since all they had were short sleeves and short pants.

She turned her head to see Nate slumped against a couple of the duffel bags, sound asleep for once. She grinned when she saw Carl next to him, looking far younger than his thirteen years as he curled in on himself in a fetal position.

It was good to see Nate getting some much-needed rest. The man had a bad habit of not getting enough sleep, feeling the need to stand guard at all times. She knew that was the protector side, but it was making for a very grouchy husband.

His condition, as well, was causing the mood changes, she was sure. He'd said as much when he'd apologized to the kids for his behavior. Since she'd never even heard of his disease that she couldn't even remember the name of, she had no idea what all was going to happen. One thing for sure was... he was going to die, and soon.

Tammy blinked her eyes furiously at the tears that threatened to spill out. It wouldn't do any good to cry, not when she knew they were all going to die sooner or later. If the signs were correct—the global economic crash, the Neos coming in and taking over—then, yeah, it was getting really close to the time when they would all die.

Or not... she remembered from the Book of Revelation how it spoke of those who would survive the end times, who would not see death and would be changed to their new bodies, their spiritual bodies. She smiled at that, hoping that would happen to her.

But Nate... a heavy feeling weighed on her then, and she remembered the first part of that dream. She'd been crying, saddened that her husband was never going to accept the Lord. That's how it seemed, anyway.

And then she'd heard the voice... and she knew with certainty that it had been the Lord. Another grin split her face when she realized that God Himself had spoken to her in a dream.

He'd told her to keep praying, to not give up hope. And He'd said that Nate would come to Him. Her grin widened.

It wasn't long before the girls awakened, but it was nearly dark when Nate and Carl finally roused. Tammy had been surprised by that—Nate was such a light sleeper that any noise would have him bolting upright, but even the girls talking didn't wake him. The only time he'd slept so soundly was when Chrissy had appeared to her.

He seemed confused when he awoke as well. Tammy had been watching him at the time while Lou talked about toys that she had at one time—probably before their parents had died. Sissy didn't seem to remember much about that time and contributed very little to memories of the past. Tammy didn't blame her; if the child's past was anything like hers, it was best left in the past.

Nate vigorously scrubbed his face with both hands, as if trying to rub his brain into action. The movement jostled Carl, who then stirred and sat up, equally confused. The kid looked around frantically, relaxing when he saw his sisters were safe and sound, then he turned to Nate and grinned.

"Looks like we both finally slept," Carl said with a yawn before stretching.

"Yeah," Nate said, though he seemed a bit disappointed that he had, as if he'd somehow failed them by giving into his exhaustion. Tammy shook her head slightly; the man was so uptight that he squeaked when he walked.

Once everyone was fully awake, they had a meal and drank some water. She wondered if Nate had noticed yet that the water bottles were staying full. It made her grin, the fact that the Lord was yet again miraculously providing for them, even for her husband who continued to deny Him.

For now.

Her heart was light as they took down their tent, packed up their "campsite" and headed out into the night.

Tammy still wondered how Nate knew where to go. She knew they had to head south, because the map they'd gotten at Gerald's showed the path stopping at the Gulf of Mexico, southeast of Tallahassee at some beach she'd never heard of. But other than that, she was clueless.

At least with a moon in the sky, she knew they were heading south, since the moon was to their left. Of course, that would change as the moon rose higher... and then there would be the nights when the moon wasn't out at all, or behind clouds. It was hard enough, walking through unknown terrain with nothing but the moon's glow to guide them, but once it was truly dark... she wasn't looking forward to that. Not at all.

She thought it made no sense to travel only at night, at least not while they were heading across the country and staying off main roads. There was little chance of being seen, unless it was by farmers and the like. From what she'd seen so far, though, most everyone had left their homes. It was like the entire country had just... vanished.

And that was a very eerie feeling.

The kids had been grumbly about walking through the night again, and Sissy had asked to be carried more than she was walking. Thankfully, both Carl and Nate had helped with the burden, though Tammy had heard Carl getting after his little sister, telling her that she was making it harder on all of them. Of course, Tammy told herself, four-year-olds didn't have guilt feelings.

Lucky them.

To pass the time, Tammy sang quietly, songs that she'd learned as a child in Sunday School. Lou joined in with several of them, and Carl surprised her when he sang "Jesus Loves Me" with them. Even Sissy knew a few of the words.

Nate seemed more stiff than usual as they sang their songs, and she wondered if it was due to him worrying about them being heard by some unseen enemy, or if he just didn't like what he was hearing. Of course, anything having to do with God and Jesus got under his skin.

But you won't hold out long! Tammy whispered to her husband in her mind with a grin.

"Can we pray?" Lou asked after they'd been walking in silence for a long while. Tammy startled at the sound of the little voice and smiled down at her, though she doubted the girl could see her, as the waning moon wasn't providing much light.

"Of course, honey. What do you want to pray about?"

Lou looked around, then back up at Tammy. "It's dark and I'm scared," she whispered.

Tammy wrapped her arm around the little girl's shoulders. "It was dark last night too," she pointed out. "You weren't scared then." Of course, last night had been a bit of an adventure for the kids, the first time they'd traveled by foot at night. They'd seemed more excited than anything. At first, anyway. Once exhaustion had taken its toll, the novelty had worn off and they had gotten cranky.

And then there was the man who'd accosted them while Sissy had been peeing. Tammy was still so angry about that, mostly because she'd let herself be grabbed. And it wasn't like she hadn't had warning, either... just before he stepped out from behind a tree, she'd sensed it, knew that something bad was coming their way. She even knew exactly where it would come from... where *he* would come from. When he'd stepped out from behind the tree, she hadn't been surprised.

And then it was as if the Spirit within her wanted to battle with the spirit within him. The man's spirit had been pure evil.

Tammy was certain he'd been demon-possessed.

When Carl had pulled the gun out from behind Nate and pulled the trigger, she'd seen it all in slow motion. The kid had a look of determination, Nate had looked like he was going to throw up, and as the bullet came toward her, she knew without a doubt that she wasn't even going to get so much as a speck of blood on her.

She'd been completely protected.

Thank You, Lord, she whispered in her mind again, for the dozenth time since the night before.

"I know," Lou said, bringing Tammy out of her thoughts, "but there's something more scary tonight."

"Yeah," Carl, who'd been walking beside them while Nate, who carried a now sleeping Sissy, walked ahead, agreed.

Carl looked around. "Feels like... I dunno. Like something's in the air. Something bad."

Tammy frowned; she'd been so wrapped up in her thoughts that she really hadn't been paying much attention to her surroundings. Truthfully, she'd gotten so dependent on Nate for being the one to notice things, to watch out for them and keep them safe, that she never really watched what was going on around her.

She tilted her head, as if listening for evil

170

whisperings. There wasn't any sound, though, as had been the case for their entire journey so far. No more planes overhead, no more cars on the roads—unless the Neos were making rounds—no more buzzing of electronics and power lines. The world had gone silent when there was no money... and Tammy couldn't say that was truly a bad thing.

As she considered the silence, she realized that the kids were right... there did seem to be an oppressive feel to the night. A clinging, almost, like a heavy blanket was being spread over them. And not a comforting one, but more like a damp wool thing that was weighing everything down and making even breathing a bit more difficult.

It reminded her of the dream she'd had, and she shuddered.

"You're right," she whispered. "There is something wrong. Something..."

"Creepy," Carl murmured. He sidled closer and Tammy wrapped her other arm around him.

"Let's pray, like Lou said," she told the kids. "Who wants to start?"

"Me," Lou said quickly. "Jesus, save us!" she whispered vehemently. Tammy's lips quirked at that as she waited for the girl to continue, but she seemed to be done.

Well, that was quick. She figured it was probably very effective too.

"Yeah," Carl whispered. "Protect us from whatever evil is around us, Lord. Something's going on. We don't know what, but just... just save us like Lou said."

"Amen," Tammy murmured. "Walk with us, Father. Send Your angels to keep us safe." She thought of

Chrissy then and wondered what she—*he*—was doing. It would be nice to have one of God's warriors by their side just then.

"Thank You for providing for us so far," Tammy continued. "You've given us shelter, food, water and safety. Your hand guided Carl's as he took out that evil creature and we thank You for that too. And also—"

"Hiya!"

Tammy spun around and jumped at the voice behind them. Her mouth widened with a grin.

"Chrissy!" she said as she impulsively hugged the angel. Realizing what she'd done, she said, "Oh! Sorry... that's probably, uh, not done, huh?"

Chrissy laughed. "Actually, it's done quite often. I get lots of hugs."

Tammy's smile widened, then she turned to introduce the kids. Chrissy spoke before she could, stepping up to the children and putting a hand on each shoulder. Lou and Carl were staring at the "woman" in awe and Tammy wondered if they knew who—or *what*—she was.

"Hello Carl," Chrissy said, then looked down at the little girl. Tammy noticed that the angel wasn't much taller than Carl and wondered what his true form was like, if it was as small, or something else. She couldn't imagine a warrior angel being five foot nothing.

"Hi Emmylou."

The child's mouth popped open then. "You know my name?" she whispered.

Chrissy nodded. "Yep. I know your whole name too. Emmylou Beatrice Eastman. And your brother is Carlson Henry Eastman. Sissy is Melissa Penelope

Eastman." She grinned. "I kinda know everything about you."

Tammy noticed the sad look that came over the angel then and knew that he/she had witnessed all that the children had gone through.

"How... how do you know all that?" Carl asked, but then he shook his head. "Never mind," he grinned. "I think I know."

Chrissy nodded. "Yep," she said again, that time making a popping sound on the end of the word. "You *do* know." She looked up then and grinned over the kids' heads. Tammy turned to see Nate standing there, staring at Chrissy with a very strange expression.

Tammy remembered then the first time she'd met the angel when her husband had awakened saying he'd had a strange dream and she'd wondered if he'd dreamed of a little blonde angel. By the look on his face, she figured he was seeing his dream come to life.

Sissy had awakened and was smiling at Chrissy, thumb in mouth as per usual. Tammy wondered how the child hadn't sucked the digit right off.

"Who... who's this?" Nate said, his voice barely above a whisper. His wide eyes glanced between Tammy and Chrissy, who laughed.

"Dude, you should see your face," she grinned. "Look like you've seen Samuel coming up out of the grave."

Tammy frowned at that; there was something familiar about what Chrissy had said, like she'd heard it somewhere before. Or read it. Chrissy looked at her over her shoulder.

"Saul and the medium, remember? Called Samuel up. The prophet was *not* happy," she said with another

173

grin and a wink.

Tammy smiled and nodded. She had forgotten more than she remembered from all her Bible studies over the years. There had been too long a period when she hadn't read it at all and she wanted to make up for that time, but it was difficult, the circumstances being what they were.

"Where did you come from?" Nate asked, again looking between the two "adults."

"From Heaven," Sissy said after pulling her thumb out of her mouth. "That's a angel."

Tammy smiled at the little girl, at her simple, if grammatically incorrect, testimony. *Out of the mouths of babes...*

She wondered what Nate was going to say, or do. The Lord knew he was as stubborn as they came when it got down to religion, or anything having to do with godly things. It was going to take the Holy Spirit Himself to get through to him.

Chrissy cocked her head, as if listening, then she winked at Tammy again. "It always takes the Spirit in these matters," she said, then turned back to Nate. Once again, Tammy was floored to hear the angel answering unspoken thoughts and knew that the Lord Himself had told Chrissy what Tammy had thought.

Chrissy didn't respond to what Sissy said, though she did walk up to Nate to pat Sissy on the back, then reached up to kiss her cheek. There was no way that the minuscule "woman" would have been able to reach the child's cheek while she was in Nate's arms, but somehow, she had.

Nate was staring at the angel like he thought he was hallucinating. Tammy wondered how long it would take for his overly suspicious nature to kick in, when he'd start demanding answers.

He started to speak, but Chrissy beat him to it. "I could use some traveling companions. Do you mind if I walk with you for a while?" She glanced around with wide eyes, then looked back at Nate with a pleading look.

"It's kinda scary out here by myself," she said. Tammy snorted out a laugh, but then bit her lip and looked away when Nate glanced her way.

She wondered if Chrissy was giving Nate big doe eyes, batting her eyelashes, playing the helpless little woman part. She must have, because Nate nodded. The man never could resist helping someone in need, Tammy thought. He had a knight in shining armor complex.

"Of course," he said. "It's not safe for a woman to be out here by herself. Especially not now." He turned and started walking again and Chrissy looked back at them and grinned.

Carl snickered as they started walking. "That's an angel, isn't it?"

Tammy was surprised by the kid's intuition, but she nodded. "Yep. Met 'her'," she said with air quotes, "about two weeks ago. Just appeared out of nowhere. Freaked me out, but I'm really glad she's here now."

He nodded. "Me too. It doesn't feel as... bad now."

"Oh, it's still bad," Chrissy said over her shoulder. She slowed her steps to let them catch up, then waved her hand in the general direction of... nowhere that Tammy could see. It was just too dark.

"The demons are out and about tonight," she said in a low voice. Tammy wondered if she didn't want

175

Nate to hear. *Probably not; he'd think she was nuts.*

"That was the oppressiveness you felt," Chrissy added. She glanced back at Nate, then back to Tammy.

"The plan was for one of them—maybe more—to possess Nathan. They want to get to him before Spirit does."

Tammy's eyes widened as she stared at the angel. "That's... that's awful," she whispered, then looked around the area with frantic eyes. "Where are—"

"Don't worry about them," Chrissy said with a dismissive wave. "They can't come near us, not with me here. Abba won't allow it. I was told to stay with you until that bonehead finally quits being such a jerk and accepts the Lord."

Tammy and Carl—even little Lou—all chuckled at the angel's words. Tammy grinned. "I'm so thankful to hear that," she said and had the awful, selfish thought that she no longer hoped Nate would accept the Lord soon... she really wanted Chrissy to stay with them.

The angel did that listening thing again, then smacked Tammy in the arm with the back of her hand. "You're bad," Chrissy said with a grin that made Tammy laugh.

They walked in companionable silence for a long while. Tammy was so relieved to have a warrior angel walking among them—almost as good as having the Lord Himself—that she couldn't stop smiling. After feeling like they were going to be attacked at any moment, it was a nice, peaceful feeling.

"Peace like a river," Chrissy murmured after a moment. Tammy nodded.

"Exactly." She cleared her throat then. "Uh, does

176

the Lord tell you everything I'm thinking?" The thought of that was a bit... worrying. *Of course, the Lord Himself knows your thoughts, dummy. What's worse than that?*

Chrissy laughed and shook her head. "Absolutely not. That would drive me bonkers. He only tells me the things I need to know, especially the questions you have that you're afraid to ask."

Tammy's smile was embarrassed. "Yeah, I'm kinda bad about speaking my mind. I mean, *not* speaking my mind," she chuckled, then shrugged. "Guess it comes from worrying that I'll say the wrong thing, ask a stupid question, or—"

"It comes from being browbeaten as a child," Chrissy said, anger in her voice. "No parent should treat a child that way. The things you went through..." She shook her head and Tammy had to swallow down the emotion crawling up her throat. She hated to think about her childhood, and especially about her father. But the man seemed to creep into her mind more and more lately.

"Unfortunately, he is answering for that now," Chrissy said. Tammy knew what the angel meant, and a deep sadness came over her at the thought. While she might have even hated her father at times—and she'd asked the Lord to forgive those thoughts—she didn't want him to suffer for all eternity.

He'd been the head deacon of their church. A "pillar" of the community, as they said. Well-respected, well-liked. Loved by all... except those he called his "loved ones." The man had appeared to be such a godly man, had even officiated several church services when the pastor had taken ill or had gone on vacation. As an adult Sunday School teacher, people had looked to him for guidance, for biblical answers.

Appearances mean nothing, Tammy thought sadly.

"It's the heart that matters," Chrissy murmured. "Abba looks at the inward person, not the persona they show the world. *He* knows exactly what they're like, what they think, and how they act behind closed doors. Only He knows the heart, and if that heart was surrendered to Him."

Tammy nodded; as an adult, she knew all that, but it was still a hard concept to swallow. She wondered how many "godly" people wouldn't be found in Heaven.

They walked for a little longer when Chrissy called out, "Hold up!" Nate had gotten quite a bit ahead of them, which Tammy thought was strange; usually he stayed close by. *He probably didn't want to hear us talking about God...*

Her husband stopped and turned toward them. When they caught up to him, Carl reached up to take Sissy and Nate shook out his arms. He'd carried the child for a long time, and Tammy knew his arms had to be aching.

"What's up?" he murmured as he rubbed one of his biceps. Tammy stepped up and took over, gaining a moan from her husband.

Chrissy glanced around and Tammy wondered if she could see into the darkness in a way they couldn't. It was likely. And that was also comforting.

"We need to take a break," Chrissy said as she looked back at Nate with a charming smile. Tammy huffed out a laugh; if she didn't know that the adorable young woman before her was really a warrior angel, she might have been worried "she" had designs on her husband.

Nate normally grumbled and griped every time they

178

had to stop—which was often, with three females in the ranks—but strangely, he just nodded. She frowned at that, again thinking that she might have been jealous over his accommodating behavior with a strange woman.

Truthfully, though, she was just thankful for the break no matter who instigated it.

Tammy asked the girls if they needed to go potty, and both nodded. She looked at Chrissy for confirmation that it was safe, and got a nod, so she took the girls by the hand and headed behind a nearby bush.

While she held Sissy so she could do her business without getting it all over her shoes, she could hear Chrissy talking to the guys. Though they were close by, her voice seemed a bit muffled, and she wondered about that; it was almost as if she wasn't meant to hear.

Lou needed her help, as well, and she was helping the girl fasten her shorts when she heard a noise that sent a chill up her spine.

A low, rumbly growl—not quite animalistic... but not quite human either.

Tammy reached into her pocket and pulled out the small handgun that Nate had insisted she carry, removing the safety like he'd shown her and chambering a round. She aimed into the blackness of the night as she stared hard in the direction the sound had come from, but she couldn't see anything. Another growl made her jump, and she almost pulled the trigger, but realized it wouldn't be wise, not without knowing what—or who—she was shooting at. It could be a dog out for a walk with a person for all she knew.

"Don't worry about him," Chrissy called out. "He's

just angry that he can't attack you."

Tammy knew the angel was talking to her, so she trusted that she knew what she was talking about and hurried the girls back to the others. She glanced at Nate, who had a rather strange expression on his face, then Carl, who looked like he was trying not to laugh. Finally, she turned back to Chrissy.

"What was that?" she asked, jerking her head toward the area the growl had come from.

"Not what... who," Chrissy said, curling her lip up. "Amon. He's the one who was sent to possess Nathan," she added, patting the man on the chest. "Good thing the Lord is on your side, big guy. That's one nasty demon."

Chrissy cupped her hands around her mouth and looked toward the area Tammy had heard the growl. "Nice try, Amon. You know you're on a short leash, jerk. Go bark at someone else."

They all laughed, though Nate looked like he was about to faint.

"So, guess we can get going again," Chrissy announced. Tammy wondered why the angel had wanted them to stop but figured she probably didn't need to know. Judging by the look on Nate's face, it had to do with him and instead, she wondered what the angel had said to her husband. She was going to ask Carl the first chance she got.

They walked for a little while longer when a faint glow in the distance caught their attention.

"What's that?" Lou asked.

Nate put his hand out to stop them going further, but Chrissy moved around him and kept right on going.

180

"It's okay," she called out over her shoulder, waving at them to join her. "They're friendlies."

Tammy figured Nate would take some convincing, but surprisingly, he started walking again, even picking Sissy up again so they could make better time.

Chapter 10

NATHAN WAS still shaking his head over the strangeness of Chrissy. His mind just couldn't comprehend all that it had been bombarded with in such a short period of time.

First, there was the fact that he'd actually dreamed of the woman weeks before. Usually, he didn't remember his dreams, but for whatever reason, he remembered that dream well. It had been... disturbing, to say the least.

When she had just appeared out of the darkness, Nathan had almost been expecting it. It was exactly what had happened in his dream, even down to the area they were walking through. And when Chrissy had waited until the girls weren't around to tell him that she'd been sent by God Himself...

He shook his head. Everyone around him had lost their freaking minds.

Chrissy was going to say something else to him, but he'd been spared whatever nonsense she was going to spew when Tammy and the girls came back. But then there was the ridiculousness of the demon...

At the time, he'd been confused, shellshocked. It was bad enough seeing someone he'd dreamed about appear in the flesh, and he'd been reeling from that when his "dream girl" decided to show just how crazy she was by telling him "God" had sent her, almost repeating what Carl had told him the morning before.

Nathan wasn't sure what was worse... knowing he'd had a "prophetic" dream, or realizing he was surrounded by insane people.

But when Chrissy had claimed a demon was off in the shadows—one that wanted to possess him, of all things—Nathan had nearly turned and run off just to get away from her. But he couldn't, *wouldn't,* do that to the kids and Tammy. Until he was incapacitated—likely in the not too distant future—then he was going to do what he could to see that they got to safety.

As they trudged along, thankfully in silence for once, he'd gone over everything that had been said. He'd had to shove down a voice inside of him that told him he should pay attention to what everyone—including the kids—were saying, that they were speaking the truth of God. And that God wanted him to accept Him. That voice belonged in a padded room, locked in a hug-me jacket along with the rest of the loonies surrounding him.

But one thing that Chrissy had said stuck with him and he just couldn't lock it away—when Tammy had taken the girls to go potty, Chrissy had turned to him with a stern frown.

"Nathan Irving Diamond," she'd said, shocking him when she used his full name. He figured Tammy must have told her what it was; for what reason, he couldn't fathom.

"You know what Doctor Riggs told you," she continued. "He gave you ten months, tops. It's been three already. Are you going to waste that precious time being a stubborn moron? Now is the time to accept the Lord!"

He'd reeled back at the vehemence coming from the tiny woman who was barely more than a girl. She was bossy, outspoken and... confusing. He wanted nothing more than to spin on his heel and stomp away, but he couldn't leave the others behind.

More than Chrissy's words, though, had been the fact that it was obvious Tammy had been talking about him to the newcomer. That aggravated him beyond measure. It felt like a betrayal, knowing that his wife was airing his medical laundry to strangers.

The worst part in all of it, though, what bothered him the most—he was pretty sure he'd never told Tammy the name of his doctor. And he knew for certain he'd never given her the exact time frame Doctor Riggs gave him for his death warrant. Rather, he'd been vague.

And then there was the nonsense about some "demon" out in the darkness. Chrissy had claimed that the creature had wanted to possess him. Nathan thought it was ridiculous; if there were such things as demons, why hadn't he ever seen one? He figured they were just humanity's excuse for doing the evil things they did. "The devil made me do it" explanations for bad behavior.

But that didn't explain the growling off in the distance, unlike any animal he'd ever heard.

Nathan was still pondering that when one of the kids asked, "What's that?"

He looked up to see a glow in the distance. It wasn't a steady light, like that of a house with a porch light burning, more of a flickering.

Like a campfire.

It wasn't like him to not notice his surroundings, especially now that there was danger on all sides. He'd been so deep in thought, though, that he wasn't even sure if they were going in the right direction.

He put his arm out to get everyone to stop until he

could investigate a way to go around the area, but the aggravating Chrissy went right around him.

"It's okay," she'd called out as she stomped off like she was joining some tailgating party, "they're friendlies."

Nathan had made a derisive sound at that; there was no such thing as "friendlies" in the time they lived. Everyone was an enemy as far as he was concerned. Other than a few people he trusted—which amounted to Tammy, Gerald and Felicia—everyone else was lumped into the "shoot first, ask questions later" category.

Since the group unanimously decided to follow the woman who wasn't much bigger than Carl, Nathan reluctantly brought up the rear. He pulled his handgun out of his waistband, wanting to have it ready just in case.

"You won't need that, Nathan," Chrissy called out from up ahead. He frowned; there was no way the woman could have seen—or heard—what he was doing. He ignored her and held the weapon against his thigh in case he needed it. He didn't want to rely on a child who'd never even shot a gun before to be in charge of their protection the next time.

But he wasn't really sure if he'd be very reliable himself. The shaking in his hand was growing worse, to the point that it never stopped. He wasn't as good a shot with his left hand, but once the shaking had gotten worse, he figured it was better than trusting his right. But then the blasted tremors had started in his left hand as well.

He sighed; with the tremors and twitching, coupled with the weakness in his leg, he was going downhill quickly. The CJD was taking its toll faster than he'd thought.

Chrissy marched right toward the campsite like she was meant to be there. She seemed to know what she was doing, though, and Nathan hoped that was the case as he ran his shaking hand over his face. He was in no shape for a shootout.

They were just about to the circle of light produced by what he now saw was a rather large fire—strange for a warm summer night, and dangerously drawing attention, Nathan thought—when Chrissy called out.

"Back again!"

There were several voices yelling, "Chrissy!" coming from the group, which Nathan could see consisted of about twelve people. All adults, mostly women.

A few of the ladies jumped up and ran over to the woman, giving her hugs. Chrissy looked over her shoulder at Tammy.

"See?" His wife laughed at the comment, while Nathan frowned, wondering what that was about.

Chrissy introduced them and the women made fools of themselves over the children. He noticed one lady wiping her eyes, presumably from tears. Nathan was still reserving judgment on the group, but he did shake hands with the men and give a nod to the ladies when it was his turn for introduction.

"Come, sit down!" one of the women said, motioning toward the ring of chairs around the fire. Nathan noticed that there were more chairs than there were people and he wondered if there were others they weren't seeing—and started worrying about an ambush. He flicked nervous eyes around the area, but it was too dark to see.

The woman named Ida spoke up then. "Sorry for

the heat from the fire. There was just a sort of... I don't know. Something weird tonight and we thought it would be comforting. Helps keep the bugs away at least."

"It was oppressive, huh?" Tammy asked as she took a chair near the kids. Nathan frowned, as the seat on the other side of her was already occupied by an older man. Disgruntled, he sat in a metal folding chair across from his wife, where he could at least watch her back, to make sure no one came up from behind.

"That it was," Ida said, while the others nodded.

"It was demons," Lou said, surprising Nathan. He didn't think the skittish child would have spoken around strangers. Tammy reached out and ran her hand over the girl's head, smiling at her.

"They're held off for now," Chrissy said. She hooked a thumb at Nathan. "They were after him, but Abba said they couldn't have him."

"Ahh," several people said, again with the head nodding. Nathan scowled at no one and everyone in general. He really hated to be talked about like he wasn't there.

"So, where are you coming from?" one of the other ladies asked his wife. Nathan couldn't remember her name.

"Indiana," Tammy answered. She waved at the children. "They're from... where are you from?" she asked Carl with a laugh.

Decatur," Carl said.

Even from across the fire, Nathan could see how his wife's eyes widened at that. His too. That was a long way from where they'd found the kids. Nearly four hundred miles by his guesstimation.

"You walked all that way?" Tammy asked and Carl nodded. *No wonder they look so bad,* he thought. It was inconceivable that three children could walk all that way and he felt a pang of regret for making them walk even further.

"I thought they were your children," one of the other women said. Tammy shook her head, a sad smile on her face.

"Well, they are now," she told the woman. Nathan sucked in a breath at her comment. There was no way he was going to adopt those kids. It was crazy to think. Especially when he wasn't going to be around for long.

And then he realized that there wasn't such thing as adoption any longer. At least, not to his knowledge. The Neos didn't seem to care much about anything having to do with families. In fact, from what he'd seen and heard, they had no use for kids, or even women, for that matter. They seemed to only be concerned with growing their army, and from what he knew, that didn't even include women. The Neos were the ultimate misogynists from what he could tell.

But the kids would be good for Tammy when I'm gone... That idea made him both wince and sigh at the same time. While he hated the idea of leaving her behind, he also wanted her to be happy, to find peace without him.

"We're going to Florida," Lou announced, making Nathan frown. He had no intention of telling these people what their plans were. He figured they'd stop for a bit, then head on their way.

"Florida," one of the women said in a soft voice that was annoying. Tammy did that too with the girls; spoke in baby talk. It always made him want to roll his

189

eyes.

"Well, that's a very long way away," the woman told Lou, then looked at Tammy. "You're walking there?"

His wife nodded and Nathan found that he was agitated that he wasn't being included in the conversation, even though he really didn't want to talk to any of them. It was a bit ironic.

"Yeah," she sighed. "Nate and I have been on the road—" she motioned to the fields around them and grinned, "—so to speak, for a few weeks now."

"And what are you up to these days?" the Ida woman asked Chrissy.

"Same ol'," the blonde answered with a grin. "Here and there. Just got back from Mexico."

"Mexico!" one of the men exclaimed. Nathan thought his name was Martin. "Always wanted to go there. Don't suppose I'll get the chance now. How's things down south?"

Chrissy shrugged. "About the same as here. Neos are all over. Got the Mexican president to make the same deal with the devil, so there goes that government. Another one bites the dust."

There was some snickering at that, probably due to the phrasing rather than the statement. Tammy turned to Chrissy.

"How do you know these people?"

"Same as you," Chrissy answered. "Was sent here to encourage them. Seems to be my lot lately," she said with a dramatic sigh, then laughed. The others laughed as well, and Nathan felt like he wasn't being told the punchline to a joke. There was something going on, something with Chrissy, and it seemed like

190

he was the only one who had no idea what it was.

The woman was strange, for sure. She said stuff that made him frown, declaring "godly" nonsense like it was verifiable truth. Appearing out of nowhere, telling him God sent her, declaring there was a demon growling in the bushes—even knowing the demon's name—yeah, she was definitely strange.

But there was some other weirdness to her as well—like how she'd kissed Sissy on the cheek when he'd held the girl in his arms. With her size, there was no way Chrissy would have been able to reach Sissy's cheek. She would have needed a stepstool or a log to stand on. Or he would have had to bend over. And yet, she'd just leaned up and reached the child without a problem. Almost as if she'd managed to grow six inches in a split second.

Nathan had barely had time to blink over that oddity when the girl-woman had dropped back down to her "normal size" and smiled up at him with a wink, like she knew what he was thinking.

And now she was talking about having just gotten back from Mexico. With commercial air flights no longer available, Nathan doubted the truth of that statement. He supposed she could have driven, but a person would have to be a millionaire to afford the fuel for such a trip. If that was the case and she had a car, then where was it now?

There were just too many questions and he meant to keep an eye on her.

She shocked him then when she turned to him and grinned, like she'd heard his thoughts. He shook his head; just something else to add to her strangeness tally.

The group chatted about nothing in particular,

then Bette, the woman Nathan had realized was married to Martin, stood up.

"Well, I think we need to get these children to bed," she announced. "We have a tent set up for them in the center of the others." She motioned to an area Nathan hadn't even noticed before. He mentally kicked himself for once again not being aware of his surroundings, and wondered if that, too, was just another facet of his disease. He hoped not; someone needed to pay attention and it sure wasn't going to be Tammy or the kids.

Just to the south of where they were sitting was a grouping of tents. If it hadn't been in the middle of what was once a farmer's pasture, Nathan would have sworn it was a campground in some state park. There were as many tents as there were people, which he also thought was odd, since he knew some of them were couples.

What Bette had just said suddenly registered with him... that they had a tent already set up for the kids. Like they'd known they were going to show up, which was impossible.

Just like so many other things had been impossible so far... Tammy praying for her leg to be healed, and it was. Praying he'd remember the day he'd had lunch with Gerald, which he had, with startling clarity. Her praying for them to find food, then finding so much they'd had to leave most of it behind. Then having the cellar lock open...

And the water—the other things might have been explained by good luck or whatever, but their water bottles never seemed to empty. He'd purposefully drank nearly all his water earlier, and yet he knew without looking that it would be full once again. There was no way any of the others had refilled it without him knowing, since he'd kept his bag with him all day.

Nathan was starting to get a headache.

"Your tent is right next to them," Bette told Tammy, though the woman at least glanced Nathan's way, as if remembering to finally include him in the conversation.

"Unless you'd all rather sleep in the same tent—"

"I wanna stay with Tammy," Sissy said with a yawn. The poor kid was exhausted, though Nathan wondered how, since she'd been carried nearly the entire time they'd been walking.

He frowned, realizing something then. It was a little shocking, knowing that his mind was starting to slip. He wasn't catching on to the things people were saying until after the fact and he wasn't noticing things in his surroundings like he should.

It was really concerning.

He shook off those thoughts and concentrated on what he'd just realized—that this group was expecting them to stay with them, for one thing. And for another, they still had a good four or five hours left of darkness which they should be making use of, traveling as far as they could while they could. Once it was daylight... he hated the idea of being out in the open.

"We need to get moving," he said, speaking for the first time since introductions had been made. Martin, sitting to his right, startled at hearing him.

"What's that?" he asked. Nathan repeated what he said, and the older man frowned.

"Nah, no need to be out on a night like this." He glanced around the area, then looked back at him, the firelight accenting his weathered face. Nathan figured the man was around fifty or so. "Too much evil out there, son."

"They're gone for now," Chrissy chimed in, though Nathan had no idea how she'd heard their conversation from across the bonfire.

Martin nodded at the woman. "Well, then, guess it's safe to travel." He looked back at Nathan. "But those kids and your woman look a bit tuckered out. Might want to stay with us a day or two and rest. Won't matter much in the grand scheme when you get to where you're going."

Nathan smirked; if only the man knew how little time he had left. There wasn't any time to waste, not with the condition worsening by leaps and bounds. A day or two could mean the difference between getting to safety or leaving Tammy and the kids to fend for themselves somewhere along the way.

He didn't tell Martin all that, but he looked back at Tammy. The woman was staring at him, a pleading look. He knew she couldn't have heard what they were talking about, but he also knew that she would know exactly what he was thinking, and how he was feeling.

Nathan sighed heavily, then nodded at her. The grin she gave him was reward enough for losing out on half a night's walking time. Tammy stood then, taking the kids with her as they followed Bette into the camp area, the other women right behind them.

Martin chuckled beside him. "Women can't ever seem to go anywhere unless they're in a pack."

"More like a herd," the man on the other side of Martin said. Nathan tried to remember his name, but nothing was coming to him. "Or a flock... they're all hens. Pecking at you, clucking all hours of the day and night, squawking—"

"I heard that!" a voice called out from among the tents. "You gotta sleep sometime, Jim." The man laughed at that, shaking his head.

"Oops," he said sheepishly, making the other men laugh.

The older man who'd been sitting next to Tammy stood then and came around to their side of the fire, sitting on Nathan's left.

"Jacob," he said with a grin. "Don't figure you remembered everyone's names."

Nathan smiled slightly, giving the man a nod. "No, I didn't," he admitted. The others reintroduced themselves then and Nathan tried to commit names and faces to memory, but he knew it was a crapshoot whether it would "stick" or not. Another problem he'd be facing. Doctor Riggs had told him memory loss was yet another one of the symptoms associated with CJD. Apparently, it was akin to dementia. *Woohoo,* Nathan thought.

"Son, you don't need to be so serious," Martin said. "You're among friends here. We don't mean you no harm. In fact, we're more than happy to share what we have with you. The good Lord had provided for us abundantly."

Nathan fought to keep his eyes from rolling up. *Great, more religious psychos.* They seemed to just team up with each other. He was starting to feel like the black sheep amongst the herd. He managed to keep any comments to himself, thankfully.

Laughter drew his attention to Jim. "Your face says it all, Nathan. 'For the love of God Almighty, don't talk about the Lord.'" His convoluted statement drew more laughter from the others.

Martin shook his head. "We don't need to tell you more than you've already been told," he said. "I'm pretty sure that wife of yours—and those kids—have already laid it on the line. Told you what you need to know, what you need to do. It's just up to you to make that decision to accept what you've been told... accept *Who* you've been told about—or not." He shrugged. "We all have to come to that fork in the road and decide which route to take."

"What's stopping you from taking the right route?" Jacob asked quietly.

Nathan sighed; he wanted nothing more than to jump up, grab his duffel and stomp off into the night. Of course, that wasn't happening any more than it would have when Chrissy showed up and turned everything upside down. Instead of doing what he wanted to, however, he told his story.

"I grew up in a Jewish home," he explained. "Synagogue every Sabbath, every feast and festival celebrated. Hebrew school. Whole nine yards," he shrugged. "My parents hated anything and everything to do with Christians. They drilled it into me night and day that Christians were delusional, that they were trying to deceive everyone else, and that I needed to stay far away from them."

He expected some griping about that, or at least some denial, the "Oh, no, Christians aren't like that," but the men surprised him by just letting him talk. It was kind of nice, truthfully.

"Once I grew up, I turned my back on my faith." He shook his head. "Not that I ever really had the faith. But I just... it all seemed like a waste of time. Worthless effort. It was all ceremony and memorizing prayers and Torah and..." he shrugged again.

"Like I said, seemed worthless. Once I was out of the house, I walked away and never looked back. Then I met Tammy and my parents were... not happy, to say the least. They'd expected me to marry in the faith and when it was clear that I wasn't going to do that, they were downright rude to my future wife. Wasn't long before I walked away from them too."

A pang of regret struck Nathan so strongly then that he almost toppled back. He rubbed at the ache in his chest, right over his heart, as he wondered what had become of his parents, if they were all right, surviving. Or if they, like so many other Jews—and Christians—had fallen victim to the Neos and their fanaticism in wiping religion off the face of the planet.

He'd probably never know.

"Anyway," he continued as he rubbed at the painful spot, "I never had a need for religion. Tammy didn't either when we first met, but after the crash... well, let's just say she 'got right'," he said with air quotes, his voice bitter.

It was quiet for a moment, and he realized the men were waiting to see if he had anything else to say. Finally, Jacob spoke up.

"Had pretty much the same experience as you, son," he said softly. "Only difference is I did marry in the faith. My Ida is the daughter of a rabbi. My father was a gabbai in a different synagogue. But we both walked away from our faith when our children were born," he shrugged, as if it was of no consequence. Nathan felt a sudden kinship with the man who was old enough to be his grandfather.

"But God..." Martin said. Jacob grinned and nodded.

"But God," he agreed. Nathan frowned, wondering

what they meant.

"But God got a hold on me," Jacob explained. "Actually, on Ida first, through a woman she'd befriended when she worked at a bank in Chicago. Unbeknownst to me at the time, Carol had been taking her lunches with my Ida and telling her about Yeshua, teaching her about the Christian ways and beliefs. Then one day, Ida gave her life to the Christ, and it was a short time later that I gave my life to Him as well." He grinned.

"That was the best decision I'd ever made."

The other men chimed in with "amens" while Nathan tried very hard to keep a neutral expression. He didn't want to offend the older men, but the Christian nonsense was getting ridiculous. Everywhere he turned, someone was spouting off about Jesus—or in Jacob's case, "Yeshua," the Hebrew name for the Christian's "God."

It seemed he couldn't go a single day without hearing "The Lord this," and "The Lord that." If he heard one more "Praise God!" he thought he might just be sick.

"Well, praise God for faithful people like Carol," Martin said, making Nathan's back teeth ache. If there *was* a God, he was sure the being was laughing at him just then.

"God does have a marvelous sense of humor," a woman's voice said, inexplicably reflecting his thought.

Nathan turned to see Chrissy walking toward them. She'd gone with the other ladies, but for whatever reason, had left them to rejoin the men. *Probably to torment me,* Nathan thought bitterly.

But then he realized she was doing that "reading

"his mind" thing again and he scowled at her, which drew a grin from the woman. She sat on the other side of Jacob, patting the old man's knee.

"It's good to see you again, Chris," the old man said.

"You'll see a lot more of me," the woman said. "And don't forget, you'll be stuck with me for all eternity."

Jacob laughed, and the others chuckled. Nathan stared at the fire, trying not to be included in the conversation. All the "God talk" was annoying him.

"Eternity is a long time," Martin said.

"That it is," Jim agreed.

"You won't notice that it's a long 'time'," Chrissy said, "especially since there isn't time in the Spiritual realm."

Nathan rolled his eyes, though he doubted anyone was looking his way to see it. The young woman spoke like she had some kind of secret knowledge, an "in" with God or something. She was one of the most annoying Christians he'd come across yet.

Chrissy laughed then and Nathan glanced her way to find her staring at him, a big grin on her face. It was a shame she was so annoying, he thought, since she was such a pretty thing. She was pale gold everywhere—her hair, her skin... *and even a glow?*

He tilted his head to the side, realizing that the woman was actually glowing. Not like she was wearing glow-in-the-dark makeup or anything—Tammy had used that stuff one Halloween and it had made her look like she'd been dead for a few months.

No, Chrissy had a light surrounding her. It reminded him of when he was a kid and he'd have a sleepover with friends, "camping" in the backyard. They'd take flashlights and freak each other out by holding them against their hands, making them glow.

It was sort of like that. And it was just as freaky.

He shook his head, wondering if he was seeing things. Maybe his eyes were acting up from staring into the fire. He turned and stared off into the darkness for a bit, then glanced back at her.

She still looked like she was on fire... from within.

"It's the Spirit," she said as she smiled at him, like she once again knew what he was thinking. He frowned at her, then looked away.

"You can't deny Him forever," Jim said. Nathan glanced his way, wondering who he was talking to and was surprised to realize it was directed at him.

"Who?" he asked, afraid he already knew the answer.

"Jesus," Martin said, while Jacob said, "Yeshua."

Nathan shook his head. He'd had enough of the God talk. He stood and ran his hands down his thighs. "Look, maybe the God thing works for you, and I'm glad it does. But it's not for me. I told you I can't stand religion—"

"Who said anything about religion?" Chrissy asked. He turned to her and saw that her head was tilted to the side like she was genuinely confused.

"All of you," Nathan said in frustration. He pointed toward the tents. "Tammy's always talking about God, about Jesus. Carl and Lou. Heck, even Sissy." He waved his hand around those at the campfire.

"And now you people, who I barely just met, are all bombarding me with the religious mumbo jumbo." He sneered. "Just leave me out of it."

"Again, who said anything about religion?" Chrissy asked. Nathan sucked in a breath, knowing she was making fun of him. *That. Was. It!* He was going to let her have it.

He pointed a finger at her. "Look—" he started, but she held up a hand and the barrage of words he was going to spew at her just sort of stopped in his mouth, like a cork had been popped between his lips.

She put up both hands. "What I mean to say is, none of us have ever said anything about religion when we've talked about Abba—about God—to you." She motioned to the men.

"Jacob told you his story, how he was brought up in the Jewish faith, and, like you, left it, only to come to the Lord later."

She turned and pointed to the tents. "Tammy returned to the Lord and has been telling you about Him. She's been praying all the time. You've seen the miracles, the answers to prayer, yourself.

"And Carl told you that God is asking for you. He's seeking you. Buddy, the Creator of the entire universe loves you and *wants* you to be with Him." She shook her head then.

"With what little time there is left, I would think you'd be breaking down Heaven's gates to get in." She stood then and started to walk off. Nathan could tell she was disgusted with him... or frustrated.

"Why don't you just show him?" Jacob said. Chrissy paused and looked back at the man, shaking her head. She glanced at Nathan.

"No, he has to come to Abba on his own."

"Show me what?" Nathan asked, but no one answered him. Jacob stared at Chrissy as she walked off into the night, then he turned back to Nathan.

"Sit down, boy," he said.

Nathan found himself obeying against his will and chalked it up to the desire to respect his elders. That's what he told himself anyway.

Jacob pointed at Chrissy, and Nathan followed his finger, eyes widening when he realized that the girl had vanished. Though it was still dark, the fire lit a large area and there was no way she would have gotten far enough to not be seen.

"What that... *girl* was trying to tell you is that none of us were talking about religion. That's man's creation," he spat. "A way to try to fit God into whatever box they want Him to fit in. God Himself said He didn't want our memorized prayers or rituals that we perform just because it's what we've learned to do." He shook his head.

"No! He wants our hearts. He wants our love. He wants us to come to Him in truth, with humbleness and brokenness. He wants us to seek Him because we love Him and need Him, not because we feel some sort of religious obligation."

Jacob stared hard at him, his dark eyes catching the firelight, making them appear as if they were glowing. It was rather eerie, and Nathan shivered.

"The Creator wants you to have a *relationship* with Him, son. He's your Father, the best Father you could ever hope for, and all He wants is for you to come home. And when you do, He'll run to meet you, ecstatic that you've finally turned away from the ugly life you've been leading and turned to the only One who can heal you. Who can—and *will*—help you get through what's left of your life. He just wants you, Nathan."

Nathan stared at the man for a long while. He startled when Martin put a hand on his shoulder. "We all had to come to that point, man," he said softly. "Some of us are more stubborn than others," he said, a tease in his voice, "but when the Lord is seeking after you, it's best you just give in. Otherwise—"

"He'll make you miserable until you do," Jim laughed. "Believe me, I know that one all too well. Oh, the stories I could tell—"

"We'll save that for another time," Jacob told the young man, fondness in his voice. He turned back to Nathan and pointed a gnarled finger at him.

"You need to think long and hard about this one thing, son—if we're wrong about God, about Yeshua—Jesus—then what harm have we caused? We've believed in Him and believed what He said, that He is God Himself, come to earth just so He could suffer and die to pay the price for our sins and that by putting our faith in Him and turning from our sins, we have the assurance of an eternity in Heaven. And on the flipside, we believe that those who refuse Him, refuse to accept the amazing gift of salvation He's offering to us... well, those people sentence themselves to an eternity of torment."

Nathan fought back a wince at that comment; it seemed like Jacob was directing it right at him.

"And due to that belief in the Lord," Jacob continued, "we've been good people, trying to do the right thing, helping others. We try not to cause anyone harm. Try to put others first, give money to the poor, feed the hungry, clothe the naked.

"If we're wrong about God and He doesn't really

203

exist, and when we die there's nothing else after our time on earth, well okay... at least we lived a good life." He stared hard at Nathan again.

"But son, the question you've got to answer for yourself is—what if we're right?"

Chapter 11

TAMMY WAS so thankful for Chrissy's reappearance and told the angel so, several times. She finally laughed and held up a hand.

"Stop. I'm not allowed to have adoring fans. That leads down the road of vanity and I sure don't want to go there. Remember what happened to Lucifer when he jumped on that one."

"Oh, yeah," Tammy cringed, shaking her head. "It's just hard to comprehend that you're an actual angel."

Chrissy laughed. "Believe it. Warrior angel, remember?" She waved at her petite figure. "I know that's really hard to believe in this form. Plus the fact that I'm just going around talking to people isn't doing much for my street cred."

Tammy and Carl both laughed at that. "Street cred," Carl snickered. "That's funny. How come you talk like that?"

"Like what?" Chrissy asked.

Carl waved his hand. "Like... like you're an American or whatever. Like a teenager, I guess."

Chrissy laughed. "Kid, I've been on the earth since... well, since before it really was the earth. Before there was dirt and sea and sky. I've walked among humans since Adam and Eve were tossed out of the garden. I speak every language known to man. It's possible I might have picked up on your slang and mannerisms," she said with a wink.

Carl's face colored as he nodded. Tammy chuckled

and wrapped her arm around his shoulders. The girls were worn out and had gone right to sleep, but Carl, in typical teenage fashion, had wanted to stay up.

They, along with the other ladies, were sitting in the biggest tent, which Ida had told Tammy had been reserved just for them when the Lord told them they were coming. Tammy had been a bit surprised by that—both that the Lord had shared that info, but also that the group would give them the largest tent. The others were barely larger than two-people pup tents. She'd tried to argue against it, saying she and Nate were fine in one of the smaller tents, but the ladies wouldn't hear it.

"We give the best to our guests," Debby, one of the youngest of the women, had said. Beth, another of the younger women, nodded.

"That's right. What we have is yours, and we insist you take the best of what we have."

Tammy finally relented but insisted they all join her inside the large tent—that surprisingly had large pillows scattered about the floor. When she'd questioned Ida about it, she'd shrugged.

"They're easier to carry than mattresses," she said. "We all use the pillows for sitting and sleeping."

Bette brought a little lantern that was a lot more modern than the one Tammy had found in Carl's GG's cellar. It seemed to be battery powered and she stared at it for a bit, drawing Bette's attention. She held it up.

"Solar powered," she grinned. "Martin and I bought a bunch of survival stuff over the years, preparing for disaster. Of course, we'd been thinking about tornadoes and the like, with the resulting power outages and whatnot. Little did we know we were preparing for the whole world to go kaput."

Ida nodded. "Jacob and I as well, had been preparing. Stocking up on food with a long shelf life. Storing water." She waved her hand toward the north. "But we had to leave most of it when we were forced to leave Des Moines."

Tammy cocked her head. "You had to leave? Why?"

Ida smirked. "Probably the same reason you and Nathan left your town—Neos coming in," she said with derision. "They'd started rounding up all the younger men, forcing them to join. They'd already gone after all the federal men and then the police. One of our boys was forced—" She choked on her words and Bette leaned over to pat the woman on the back. Beth also sobbed and Jasmine hugged the girl.

"Beth's husband was conscripted by them too," Bette explained to Tammy before looking at Beth.

"He'll be fine," Bette told the woman. "We're praying for him, right?" She looked at Ida. "We're praying for Rodney, too. The Lord's got them in His capable hands."

Ida nodded, then wiped at a tear. "I know," she sniffed. "It's just hard to think of what he's going through." Beth nodded in agreement.

Ida glanced at Tammy. "Rodney never accepted the Lord," she said. "Stubborn, like your man. But he'll come around," she said with assurance. "They both will."

Tammy's eyes widened. She hadn't told the women anything about Nate not being a Christian, or that he'd been stubborn, refusing to hear anything to do with witnessing. She looked at Chrissy with a raised brow.

The angel chuckled and held up her hands. "Don't look at me. I'm just the messenger when I'm told to be."

Ida laughed. "Oh, that's right," she said as she patted Tammy's knee. "You wouldn't know about Chris here coming to us last week and telling us to prepare for you to join us. She told us all about Nathan and how we needed to be girding our loins, whatever in the world that means." That drew snickers from the other women.

"Back when men wore robes," Chrissy explained with a smile for the older woman, "if they were going to run or do some hard work, they'd pull the robe up between their legs and tie it around their waist. Sort of made a pair of shorts out of it."

"Ah," Ida said with a nod. "Always wondered what that meant." She looked back at Tammy. "So, I guess that meant that we were in for some hard work in witnessing to your man out there." She motioned toward the direction of the campfire.

"But my Jabob's got a hold on him right now, and that man will chew the boy's ear off until he knows everything there is to know about Jesus," she finished with a smile.

Tammy returned it, then sighed. "I sure hope he gets through to him." She glanced at Chrissy. "I've been praying all the time for him, like you said."

"Me too," Carl said proudly. He sent a sheepish look to Tammy. "Well, since we met up with Tammy and Nate, I've been praying... for everything and everyone," he admitted. "I, uh, sorta forgot about God after my GG died." He, too, sounded choked and Tammy wrapped her arm around his shoulders again.

Chrissy nodded. "That's easy for humans to do, for some reason," she said sadly. "Whenever things are going good you all turn away from your faith. Or when things are bad, you turn away, thinking He doesn't care enough about you to keep you from the bad stuff happening. It hurts Abba, by the way. He always wants to hear from His children."

The group was quiet, but then Jasmine, the youngest of the ladies, spoke in a soft voice. "I never forgot about God," she said. "He's the only One who will listen to me. Who really hears me."

"That's cuz you never talk!" Ida said with a laugh. She leaned across the circle and gave Jasmine's knee a soft slap. "We're all here for you, gal. If you want to talk, then talk! The Good Lord knows we all do enough of it, especially Bette. Might be nice to hear someone else chattering for a change."

Bette huffed out a gasp of outrage and crossed her arms over her chest. "Now, you listen here," she bit out. "I do *not* talk that much, and I don't appreciate you telling Tammy here that I do. That's just not right. I mean, she doesn't know me, doesn't know anything about me, but you're telling her right off the bat that I'm some sort of chatterbox. It's just not true, and I think that—"

"See what I mean?" Ida said to Tammy as she flipped her hand toward Bette. The other woman's mouth snapped shut as the others snickered, and she started to say something else, but thought better of it. After a moment, she started laughing.

"Okay, maybe I do talk a lot," she muttered, drawing even more laughter.

Juana—who Tammy found out had recently been married to Jim in a ceremony performed by Jacob that Ida said wasn't technically legal, but it was "good enough in God's eyes"—started telling the group about her fears of getting pregnant. She asked for the other ladies' advice. That's when Chrissy stood.

"Well, that's not a conversation I need to be included in," she said with a laugh. She turned to Tammy. "Abba just told me to talk to your man anyway," she said with a wink. "Keep praying."

Ida looked at Juana. "We'll get back to your problem later, honey." She reached out and grabbed Tammy's hand on one side and Bette's on the other. "Grab a hand and let's pray for Tammy's husband," she told the others. "And then you all are going to have to help me get up off this pillow so I can go pee."

That caused more snickers, but Ida started praying for Nathan to accept the Lord, for his heart to be softened, for him to realize that God loves him. Bette added her prayers for Nathan to realize that God was true, that His Word never failed, and that time was short. The other women prayed for much the same and then it was Tammy's turn.

"Lord—" that was all she got out when her voice caught, and tears filled her eyes. She felt such a great burden come on her then, as if a heavy weight had been dropped on her shoulders and she leaned forward, sobbing.

"Please, Father," she cried out. The words wouldn't come as she continued to sob. Ida's hand tightened around hers and she felt Jasmine's head lean on her shoulder. The woman was crying, as well.

Tammy continued to cry silent tears for several minutes before she gasped as she *felt* the Holy Spirit rise up within her, taking over where the words failed her.

"*...the Spirit Himself intercedes for us with groanings too deep for words...*"

The scripture filled her mind, as if being spoken by the Father Himself. Tammy grinned through her tears as she tried to get some control of her emotions, but it seemed an impossible task. There was just so much... hope, suddenly.

It was an indescribable feeling, like she was listening as God Himself prayed for her, for Nathan. It made her sob even harder, though it was now with gratitude.

A part of her expected the other women to say something, to start praying again, but they were silent. Tammy realized with some surprise that she could also feel their prayers as well, as if all were praying in unison. It seemed to amplify the awareness she felt of the Holy Spirit within her, and she gasped again.

It was overpowering. Overwhelming.

Just as the feeling became too much, it suddenly stopped. Tammy sucked in a breath and as one, the women all whispered, "Amen," then all fell silent again.

"Wow," Ida breathed after a long while. Tammy glanced at her as the woman shook her head. Ida smiled at her, then released her hand to lay her hand on her shoulder.

"Been a Christian for nearly sixty years," she said with another head shake, "but I've never had an experience like that before."

"Me either," Bette said, sounding just as awed. The others murmured in agreement as Tammy wiped her face. Jasmine handed her a piece of cloth, which Tammy took with a grateful nod. She blew her nose, then started to hand it back to the girl. She laughed as she changed her mind, tucking it in her pocket.

"I'll wash that before I give it back to you."

211

Jasmine shook her head. "Don't return it. We have plenty of cloths."

"Yep," Beth agreed.

"We use them for everything from snot rags to toilet paper," Debby added. Tammy made a face and Jasmine laughed.

"Don't worry; the one I gave you was brand new." She shrugged. "Since we can't easily wash clothes and all, we just bury the rags we use for, uh, wiping."

Tammy laughed in embarrassment at having her thoughts brought out in the open, but then she sighed as she looked out the door of the tent.

Glancing back at the other women, she said, "Well, now we just have to wait for the Lord to knock some sense into that hard rock sitting atop my husband's shoulders."

NATHAN WASN'T sure what to think of Jacob's testimony, and he sure didn't know what to say to the question the old man had asked, the one that kept ringing through his head:

What if the Christians ARE right?

He'd stayed quiet after Jacob finished talking, listening as Jim and Martin gave their own testimonies. He'd been surprised to hear that Jim had accepted the Lord himself just a few weeks earlier. Nathan thought that was strange, because the man seemed to have a lot of knowledge of Jesus and all. He spoke the "language" at least.

Chrissy hadn't returned, and Martin seemed to mirror Nathan's thoughts when he asked if the others thought they'd see her again.

"When the Lord wills it," was all Jacob had said.

Jim had nodded. "Yeah, whenever He thinks we need some more encouragement."

"Or a butt kicking," Jim added with a laugh.

The men chatted for a long while, though Nathan didn't add much to the conversation, choosing instead to stare into the flickering flames. He had never been much for small talk, and the churchy stuff the guys were discussing sure wasn't his choice for topics.

The camaraderie was nice, though, he had to admit to himself. It was a good change, being with men. All he'd had for months had been Tammy's companionship. While he loved his wife, he'd missed having Gerald around to talk things through with and it made him want to get to Florida even more desperately.

After a while the men all fell silent, each staring at the fire, or into the darkness. Nathan didn't like to look out past the fire's light. Regardless of his lack of belief in God, there was one thing that he had figured Chrissy said was true... some sort of evil seemed to be out there.

He shuddered as he recalled the girl's words, that a demon—or maybe plural—wanted to possess him. Nathan still felt that was ridiculous, but he couldn't deny that there was *something* out there, a presence like he'd never felt before. And it was rather terrifying.

What bothered him more than anything else, he supposed, was not having a... *being* to fight. Something "real," a man or a beast or whatever in front of him that he could shoot or punch. Dealing with invisible entities wasn't high on his list of things he wanted to do.

And then he told himself he was being ridiculous. *There is no such thing as demons, or invisible entities, or... whatever.*

Jacob cleared his throat then, startling him out of his thoughts. "So, Nathan... the kid said you're heading to Florida?"

Nathan nodded. "Yeah. Got a friend who's ahead of us, going that direction. Left a note that we needed to follow them." He shrugged. "Supposed to be some sort of community there, away from the Neos."

Jacob nodded. "Heard about them popping up here and there," he said. "We came across one ourselves on our way south from Des Moines. Wasn't what we wanted for ourselves, though."

Nathan frowned. "How's that?" It seemed to him that anyone would be happy to find some like-minded people they could hole up with. Safety in numbers and all that. Especially people as old as Jacob and Ida.

"They weren't believers," Jacob said simply. "Didn't share our values. Couldn't see living with them, watching all the goings on. The outright sin. Might as well have stayed in the city if we wanted to compromise our beliefs like that."

That shocked him, though Nathan kept his thoughts to himself. He knew whatever came out of his mouth would likely be offensive. But he could feel that anger boiling under the surface again, that need to lash out and tell Jacob what an idiot he was, how he should have taken whatever opportunity came his way to keep him and his wife safe...

He fought those thoughts back. It was difficult, though, because it was almost an unreasonably strong sense of needing to get his point across, in any way possible. He clenched his fists and gritted his teeth, forcing the words to stay in his head and not come of his mouth.

It's the CJD, he told himself. Doctor Riggs had warned him of behavioral changes, among other things. The tremors were bad enough, he thought, and especially the leg weakness when they had so far to walk every day. But adding in emotional outbursts... he was a wreck.

And the thought entered his head once again that he should just take himself out of the equation and be done with it. It would make things easier on Tammy. She could make it to Florida on her own without having to drag an incapacitated, emotionally charged disaster along.

He shook those thoughts away and forced himself to calm down. *Deep breaths. Deep breaths. In... out...*

"You okay, son?"

Nathan startled and looked at Martin. The man nodded his way. "You look like you want to tear something apart. Something got your goat?"

Nathan hissed the breath he'd been holding out through his teeth, then jerked his head from shoulder to shoulder, cracking his neck.

He glanced at the men who were all staring warily at him. "Sorry," he muttered. "I... sometimes I get, uh, I get... I lose control of my emotions," he said helplessly.

Jacob was staring intently at him and it unnerved Nathan, but he forced himself to hold the man's gaze. Finally, the old man nodded.

"Seems you've got something going on you're not telling us."

"Because it's none of your business," Nathan snapped, then instantly regretted it. There wasn't any reason to be mean or rude to the men, even if they were nosier than his mother and her sisters.

"Sorry," he said again, shaking his head. "That's what I mean," he added with a wave. "The emotions get out of control sometimes."

Jacob put his hand on Nathan's shoulder. "That's not a burden you have to carry by yourself, son." He nodded toward the others. "Tell us what's going on, so we know how to pray for you."

Nathan closed his eyes and sighed heavily. He was so tired, drained, and had no fight left in him to argue against all the "God talk." Instead, he found himself doing as Jacob asked.

"I have CJD—Creutzfeldt-Jakob disease," he admitted. Jacob sucked in a breath and Nathan looked at him. "You know what it is?" It was a rare disease and not many had heard of it.

The old man nodded. "Lost several in my family over the years to it." He looked at the other men. "There's literally a one in a million chance of getting it, but those of us Jews who have North African heritage are more likely."

Nathan smirked. "My grandparents were Libyan Jews."

"My family as well," Jacob said with a smile. "We are probably cousins."

Despite the topic and Nathan's bouncing emotions, he forced himself to return the smile. "Possibly are," he agreed. He glanced back at the others.

"Anyway, it's fatal and the disease is already progressing." He held out his shaking hand. "Tremors,

216

leg weakness, tics... I'm already a mess and it's just going to get worse."

The men were silent for a long while, but then Jim spoke. "I had a fatal disease too," he admitted. Nathan frowned at his use of the word "had," but he didn't comment.

"Alcoholism," he said with a shrug. "Up until a month ago, I was falling down drunk all the time. When the economy took a dive and I couldn't afford to buy booze, I turned to... other stuff," he admitted with a shudder. "You don't want to know what all I drank. Stuff that should have killed me, that's for sure." He smiled at Martin.

"But then I came across Martin and Bette. Well, they came across me, I guess."

Martin laughed as he clapped the young man on the back. "Tripped over him, actually. He was passed out in an alley that I'd ducked down to avoid a Neos patrol. Fell right over him. It was the Good Lord's blessing I didn't break something."

Jim shook his head. "Instead of yelling at me—or worse, ignoring my existence like most people did—Martin pulled me up, dusted me off, then took me home with him."

"That took a while," Martin said with another laugh. "It was more stumbling than walking, but once we got him in the house and Bette got some food into the boy, he started to sober up."

"And then you laid Jesus on me," Jim laughed, shaking his head. "Both of them. Tag teamed me even. I didn't stand a chance."

"Satan didn't stand a chance, son," Martin said quietly. Jim smiled and nodded, then looked back at

Nathan.

"That night, I got right with the Lord. It was the hardest—and easiest—decision I'd ever made." He grinned at the look Nathan gave him.

"Hardest, cuz I knew if I got right with God, I'd have to change my 'evil ways'," he said, crooking his forefingers. "But easiest, cuz once I asked Jesus to forgive me and take over my life, that's exactly what He did." He shook his head. "I never even thought about drinking again from that moment on."

"The Lord doesn't want you to clean yourself up before you come to Him," Martin said. "He wants you to come, just as you are. He'll do the cleaning for you."

Jim nodded at the man, then looked back at Nathan. "If the Lord could heal a broken, beaten down man who had resorted to drinking hairspray and antifreeze just so he could avoid living in reality, then I know He can heal you of this... this disease you have."

The other men said "amen," while Nathan frowned. He didn't comment, though he wanted to tell them they were all crazy. Even if there was a God, why in the world would He heal him, if He even could?

Once again, Nathan kept his thoughts to himself. It wasn't easy, though, when he was still fighting down the urge to yell at them, to tell them they were all morons believing in some fairytale. The feeling was growing stronger by the moment, and it was nearly impossible not to lash out.

"Son, you've got a demon messing with you," Jacob said suddenly. Nathan blinked a few times and looked at the old man, but he wasn't looking at him... he was looking behind him. Nathan stood and spun around to see what Jacob saw, but there wasn't anything there.

Jacob pointed somewhere above Nathan's head. "He was just there, muttering something to you," he told him, shaking his head. He glanced at the other men. "Don't have that happen too often, seeing in the Spirit like that. Kinda scary."

Martin and Jim stared at the area behind Nathan. "Don't see anything," Martin said, and Jim shook his head in agreement.

"Not there now," Jacob said, rubbing his jaw with his hand.

Nathan wondered just how crazy the old man was, but then he realized that he no longer had the desire to tell him that he thought he was insane. The anger, the need to lash out at the men, had fled.

Jacob pushed himself to a stand then. He put a hand on the back of his chair and lifted the other one above his head.

"Father God, in the Name of Your precious Son, Yeshua, I cast out all demons here. I bind their evil whisperings and all devices they're using to keep Nathan from hearing You, from turning to You. Send them back to the Pit where they belong, Father. Amen."

The other men added "amens" as well, though Nathan stared at them all like they might be on the verge of sprouting wings or something. But he couldn't deny that he felt better, not as angry.

"They're gone again," a woman's voice called out. Jacob turned as he dropped his hand and grinned.

"Could have used your help a moment ago," he told Chrissy as she walked back into the ring of light surrounding the fire. Nathan frowned again, wondering where she'd been, where she'd just come from, and why in the world Jacob would think she would be any kind of help.

With demons, he snorted to himself. Ridiculous.

The girl shrugged. "Like I said, they're gone."

"Thanks to you," Jacob said. Chrissy grinned at the old man. The smile fled, however, when she looked at Nathan.

"You have no more time left," she said.

He frowned in response. "What does that mean?" He knew that he wasn't close to dying; at least, not by CJD standards. There was still a course of symptoms he had to go through before he got to that point. He swallowed hard at the thought. Death wasn't something he'd ever really been afraid of; after all, he believed after he died, that was it. Just... nothing.

Dying, however... that scared the life out of him. *Literally,* he thought with bitter humor.

Chrissy didn't seem inclined to answer and just gave him a sad shake of her head as she turned to walk off toward the tents. The men watched her go, then Martin spoke.

"She means that there comes a time when we're given our last chance to get right with God, to accept Jesus." He sighed heavily. "I guess that's the point you're at now."

"Yep," Jacob said, shaking his head in much the same way Chrissy had. "Son, you have no more time to waste. You can't keep thinking you can make a decision later, that there's still time. We don't know how much time we have." He looked up at the starry sky. "For all we know, a meteor could be coming our way and drop on our heads." His eyes found Nathan's again.

"Now is the time you have to decide—do I believe in God? Do I accept Jesus as my Savior? Accept all that He did for me and know that I'll spend all of eternity in Heaven with Him?"

He pointed a gnarled finger at Nathan. "Or do you get mired in your prideful stubbornness and spend eternity in suffering and torment? There are only two choices, son. You'd best make the right one."

With that, all three men stood and walked off toward the tents, leaving Nathan standing next to the fire, staring after them.

He sighed then, knowing he'd been ostracized from the group and a sudden wave of loneliness swept over him. It was more than just feeling like he was alone by the fire—he had a sense of being alienated. As if he was the only person in the world in that moment.

Nathan suddenly felt tired, exhausted. He slumped further into the uncomfortable metal chair and went back to staring into the fire, contemplating... everything.

Now that they'd found others who weren't on the Neos' side, who were just trying to stay under the radar, he wondered if it wouldn't be better to stay with them. It would sure be easier on Tammy and the kids. And him, if he were being truthful. Walking hundreds of miles over the next few months was looking more and more like an impossible task.

Maybe I should just leave. That thought was quickly followed by a sense of leaving permanently. The suicidal ideas were coming more and more frequently, and Nathan was starting to think they had merit.

Why go through whatever time he had left as a burden to others? Lashing out as his emotions ran

221

wild, succumbing to the inevitable paralysis, eventually forgetting everything and everyone.

It was certainly no life to look forward to.

He leaned forward and put his elbows on his thighs as he stared deeper into the fire. Tammy now had the kids and the others, if she chose to stay. She really didn't need him any longer. While Jacob was old, Martin and Jim were both young enough to protect them. And Carl had proven that he wasn't afraid to step up when needed. Heck, the kid hadn't hesitated shooting that creep in the woods, hadn't balked... and hadn't had any regrets afterward.

Of course, he told himself, he could always teach Tammy and the others how to shoot, to defend themselves, before he... left. His last act, training whoever needed it. At least he'd leave the earth having done *something*.

He sat there contemplating everything that ran through his mind, all the pros and cons. Truthfully, he couldn't think of any cons to an early death, dying before the symptoms got so much worse. It just made more sense and if he were going to do it, it had better be soon, before he got too incapacitated.

Nathan reached down and plucked a piece of dry grass near his shoe. He turned the blade over in his hands, wondering if Kentucky had been through the drought like Indiana. Traveling at night gave them no sense of their surroundings, if they were walking through green fields, or dead dry ones. He guessed the latter; their feet seemed to crunch with every step. Two years with no rain made everything brittle. Fragile.

He tied the dry blade into a knot and tossed it into the fire, watching as it sparked and disappeared in just seconds. Nathan sighed... *just like life*. You lived your life thinking everything was fine, then circumstances changed—like the drought for the grass, or the crash for the rest of the world—and suddenly POOF, whatever you once believed is no longer true.

And then you had no idea what to believe.

"Believe in Me..."

Nathan startled. His heart started to pound as he realized he'd heard a voice in his head. It wasn't a voice he recognized, like he'd been hearing his Papa speaking, which happened at times. Memories, really.

"Nathan, you know what you are to be doing. That is not how Mama and I raised you..."

"Do not disappoint us, Nathan. We have high expectations for you."

This voice was much different. Stronger, yet softer. Compelling, without being demanding.

He shook his head. "Great, now I'm starting to hallucinate." He didn't think that was one of the symptoms of his disease, but truthfully, he'd stopped listening to the litany of all the things that he could expect after Doctor Riggs said "paralysis." That was the one thing that terrified him the most—not being able to move.

Thinking of the paralysis, Nathan suddenly felt antsy. Like he was already being trapped inside his own body. He stood, feeling the need to move while he could. He paced back and forth, then circled the fire.

Kicking dirt at the flames as he walked around, he thought it was careless for the men to have left the fire burning, especially with the dry grass in the area. He figured they'd probably expected him to take care of it. He kicked a little more dirt, watching as the flames flickered and started to die back, but then he realized he didn't want the darkness. Not while he was alone.

Nathan glanced out toward the area Chrissy had claimed there'd been a demon, then turned and looked back where he'd been sitting, where Jacob had claimed to see one as well. He saw nothing but darkness.

But there was something about the darkness that night. It wasn't just the night, or the fact that it was darker since the moon had yet to rise. This was more than that... it was a darkness that seemed to surround him. Wanting to pull him into its depths.

He shuddered and realized he was being ridiculous. "I'm not some kid, afraid of the dark," he muttered. "Get it together."

The self-talk didn't help, and he paced some more, casting wary glances into the black beyond the ring of the fire's light. He paused when he thought he saw movement and held his breath, staring for a long while into what he thought was a wooded area. Though it was too dark to see, he thought he could make out the shapes of trees swaying in the wind.

He frowned; there wasn't any wind. Not even a breeze.

Staring harder at the area, his eyes widened when he realized that the trees *were* moving, except they weren't swaying in the breeze. They were walking.

"I... I... uh..." Nathan didn't know why he was trying to speak; it wasn't like there was anyone around to hear him. Or to answer. He shook his head again, trying to clear it, this time hoping he was having a hallucination.

The "trees" continued to walk, though they made no sound. As he concentrated on the area, his eyes seemed to focus better, to see what was truly there.

And then he wished he hadn't.

Huge creatures, massive forms of blackness moving about. *No, prowling...* They reminded him of apex predators seeking a kill—searching through the prairie grass, looking for a rabbit or some other rodent.

Or a human...

Nathan's breath left him in a whoosh as he realized that Chrissy's words—and Jacob's—were true. There were demons surrounding them. He struggled to come to grips with that, arguing with himself that he was being ridiculous, but he couldn't deny what he was seeing, and he knew without a doubt that it wasn't a hallucination.

But the one thing that struck him most, and hardest, as he stared toward the creatures—if there was such a thing as demons, then that meant...

There was such a thing as God.

Chapter 12

T HAT WAS QUICK," Ida said as Chrissy walked back into the tent. The angel nodded. Tammy frowned. She looked... sad.

The "girl" sat down and stared at the floor for a few minutes. No one said anything, but all stared warily at her. Tammy knew they were all thinking the same thing she was... did angels have human emotions such as sadness?

And, if so, what was so bad that one of the Heavenly Host would feel that way?

After a long while, Chrissy sighed and looked up, staring at Tammy. She still didn't speak, and Tammy squirmed a bit under her scrutiny. Chrissy shook her head.

"Nathan is... very stubborn."

Tammy huffed out a laugh. "Yeah, that he is," she admitted. "I always said that he'd out stubborn a mule."

She expected Chrissy to laugh, as the others did, but she just continued to stare at her, that same sad expression on her face. Tammy frowned and tilted her head.

"What?" she asked. "What's wrong?"

Chrissy pursed her lips, then sighed again. It was a very human thing to do, Tammy thought, and wondered if the angel spent more time in the earthly realm than she did in the heavenly one.

"I was told that Nathan's time is up."

Tammy's eyes widened at that, as panic engulfed her. "His time... his *time* is up?" she squeaked out. "What do you mean? Like, he's gonna die already? I thought he had a year or—"

"Not that," Chrissy said with a head shake. "It's worse, though. Abba has said that he's been given his last chance to turn to Him. There are no more chances."

There were gasps and "Oh nos" from the women, but Tammy didn't make a sound. Didn't say a word. She just sat in stunned silence as she considered what the angel was telling her.

God Himself has decided that my husband is out of time...

She numbly realized that Ida was rubbing her back, trying to console her. Tammy wanted to shrug off the ministrations, wanted to be left alone in her misery, but she was frankly paralyzed with pain.

It had been hard, having Nate admit to her that he was dying of a disease she'd never even heard of. But she'd known that if she could just get through to him, just get him to realize that Jesus was real and that He loved him enough to die for just him, that she'd see the man again on the other side. She had clung to that and had prayed every night as they'd walked across unknown and unseen terrain.

And during the day, as she'd read her Bible, she'd prayed. Cried out to God to save her husband, to bring him to his knees and soften that stubborn heart. Over and over, she'd begged the Lord for that.

She'd dreamed of God Himself telling her that Nate would be saved. She was sure of it, sure that she'd truly heard Him speaking.

Then earlier, when the women had all prayed with her and they'd felt the Holy Spirit moving so strongly among them, she'd just known that her prayers were finally going to be answered.

But now...

Tammy shook her head. *No, this isn't right!* She sucked in a deep breath, letting it out slowly. It wasn't right; in fact, it was all wrong. She *knew* God was going to answer her prayer, *knew* that He was going to get through to Nate, *knew* that her husband was going to be saved.

She'd believed it with all her heart.

"Father," she called out suddenly as she tilted her head skyward, "I'm still believing You'll get through to Nate. I have faith, Father. Please don't let him get away. Bring him to You! Save him, Jesus, I'm begging You!" With that, she broke down into sobs once again as Ida pulled her into an embrace.

She heard the other women calling out to God again, as well, repeating their prayers from earlier. Begging the Lord to change His mind, to have just a tiny bit more patience with Nate. They cried, pleaded, and quoted God's own words to Him while Tammy's heart shattered in the arms of a woman she'd just met.

"Wait!" Chrissy said, interrupting the prayers. Tammy lifted her head from Ida's shoulder and turned to look at the angel through her tears. Her eyes widened when she saw that she... *no, HE...* was truly an angel then, a very large one, glowing blue and holding an extremely large sword as he stood with his feet apart, as though ready to do battle.

He looked around at the women and grinned. "Abba has heard your prayers," he told them. "And He has given Nathan one last invitation to come to Him."

229

He looked at Tammy, giving her a crooked grin.

"And Nathan accepted."

NATHAN FELL to his knees as soon as the realization that God was truly real struck him. He didn't stop there, but put his forehead to the dry, hard ground and sobbed.

"Forgive me, Lord," he cried. "I'm a stubborn man, I know that. Please forgive me for not accepting You before. And I know You said I was out—" the words caught in his throat then and he swallowed hard, "—that I was out of time," he continued, choking on the words.

"But from what Tammy's told me, You're a merciful God. Please, please, Lord, have mercy on me. I don't deserve it, I know, but I swear to You, whatever time I have left will be spent in praise of You and telling others about You. Just please, Father God, please forgive me."

He stopped praying and remained in his hunched position, making mud in the dry earth with his tears. There was no answer, no voice from Heaven telling him that "all is forgiven," and Nathan wondered—and worried—that he'd been too late. That God had decided he wasn't worth forgiving.

Nathan couldn't say that he'd blame Him.

It was a long time before he moved from his position, but that was just to sit back on his heels. He kept his head bent to the ground, not wanting to lift it to see the demons closing in around him. He was sure that was going to be his lot with what was left of his life—to be possessed by a demon.

He couldn't let that happen, he realized. If he were

possessed, who knew what he might do to Tammy, to the kids. While he knew next to nothing about demons, he knew without a doubt that the creatures he'd seen prowling around the area were terrifying... and that they absolutely hated humans. Of that, he had no doubt. The hatred oozed off them like a sticky tar.

Nathan reached into the back of his waistband and pulled out the nine-millimeter, quickly chambering a round before he thought twice about it. But then he paused, wondering if he should at least tell Tammy goodbye, tell her he loved her.

Kiss her one last time.

He shook his head, knowing if he talked to his wife, she'd know what he had planned and would talk him out of it. Nathan knew she'd do anything to stop him, and he wasn't sure if he was strong enough to resist. He couldn't have that. He couldn't put her in danger. The thought of hurting Tammy, or the kids, terrified him.

He steeled himself, knowing what he had to do.

A flash of light caught his eye and he stared at the gun in his hand. While he'd been needlessly begging God for forgiveness, the moon must have started to rise, as its glow caught the weapon, making the black metal appear blue. He turned it over, putting it into his left hand. He no longer trusted his shaking right hand to be able to do the job properly.

He lifted the weapon and held his breath. "I really am sorry, God," he whispered. "Please take care of my wife."

"I wouldn't do that, if I were you."

Nathan dropped the gun and turned his head to

see... something completely indescribable. A huge creature—that he suddenly realized had been the source of the blue glow—stood behind him, even bigger than the demons he'd seen earlier. But he somehow knew this was no demon.

Angel...

"At your service," the angel said with a sweep of the massive sword he held. The thing had to be ten or twelve feet long, Nathan thought. And the angel himself stood at least two stories tall.

"Zadkiel, at your service," he told Nathan, then grinned. "Otherwise known as Chrissy."

Nathan blinked a few times. "Chris... Chrissy?" he choked out. "You mean, the little—"

"Blonde bombshell?" the angel asked with a crooked grin. "Yep, that's me." He pointed his sword in the direction the demons had been. "But that form isn't conducive to fighting the enemy." He then swept the sword in front of him, down his body. "This one works a bit better."

Nathan turned to look at the area where the demons had been but didn't see the evil creatures any longer. He supposed that was a bit of a relief, but his heart ached too much to feel it. It was especially hard, knowing that he'd have to spend eternity with the terrifying things.

The angel snickered and he glanced back up at him but was surprised to see he'd changed back to the "Chrissy" form. Nathan shook his head, thinking at how very strange his life had gotten in just a short time.

"You *want* to spend eternity with them?" Chrissy said as she—he—pointed to the area where the demons had been.

"Well, no, of course not," Nathan said with a scowl. "But—"

"But nothing," Chrissy said with a shrug. She grinned. "Oh, maybe you don't know, but Abba—God— decided to forgive your stubborn self after all."

Nathan blinked a few times, trying to process what he'd just been told. "But... but I... I didn't—"

"What, you thought you'd see a burning bush, or something?" Chrissy interrupted with a smirk.

Nathan frowned. "Well, no, but I thought I might... feel different, I guess."

The angel actually rolled her eyes and crossed her arms over her chest. "You humans always want the big dramatics. What's up with that?" She shook her head. "Seriously, I have an 'in' with Abba, and He said you've joined Team God," she added with a grin, then motioned to the forgotten gun still in his hand.

"So, put that thing away and get busy doing what you promised you'd do—praise Him and tell everyone you meet about Him." She smiled, then turned back into the terrifyingly huge angel in the blink of an eye. Nathan did just that... he blinked, rapidly.

"Gotta go," the angel named Zadkiel said, his deep voice booming. He glanced up, then looked back at Nathan with a smile. "Have a choir session." Zadkiel grinned at Nathan's expression.

"Whenever a human accepts the Lord, the angels get to sing. It's pretty cool, and if you listen hard, you might just hear it." With that, he vanished.

Nathan was still staring up at the sky, hoping to see a glimpse of... something, when the others came running from the tents. He was still kneeling on the ground, and he quickly tucked his weapon under his leg just as Tammy reached him, nearly knocking him sideways as she tackled him to hug him around the neck.

"You're saved!" she shouted in his ear, sounding ecstatic, though she was crying. Nathan wrapped his arms around her.

"I'm forgiven," he said, still in awe. It had been just seconds since the angel told him as much, and he was still trying to process it. But he wasn't going to doubt it—if Chrissy, or Zadkiel, whatever, told him it was so, that "Abba" had declared it, then Nathan was going to trust that it was truth.

"You are," Tammy laughed. She moved aside then as Carl came up and threw himself at Nathan. He laughed as he hugged the kid he'd grown fond of in such a short period of time.

"Welcome to the family!" Carl said with just as much enthusiasm as Tammy'd had.

Nathan realized he was going to be forced to stand as the others came forward. He grabbed the gun as he stood and held it to his thigh while he awkwardly hugged everyone with one arm.

He glanced down when he felt a tug and saw Carl give a slight jerk of his head and knew the kid wanted to take the weapon from him, probably to keep it out of sight from the others. He nodded once and released it to him, watching as the kid tucked it into the back of his pants and pulled his shirt down over it. Nathan gave him a grateful smile. The last thing he wanted to do was be chewed out by his wife for what he'd planned on doing.

Jacob walked up to him then and startled Nathan

when he laid his hands on his head. The old man closed his eyes and tilted his head back.

"Heavenly Father, thank You for Your infinite patience and merciful love in waiting for our new brother in Christ to accept You. And now, I ask that You fill him with Your Holy Spirit. Pour the Spirit upon Nathan as he goes about doing Your works and sharing Your Word. Give him the boldness he needs now to stay strong in the faith. Amen.

For some strange reason, Nathan started laughing. Jacob stepped back and smiled at him, then started speaking in Hebrew. Nathan startled when he realized he understood the man perfectly, though he hadn't heard the language since he'd been a boy in school.

"The sound of joyful shouting and salvation is in the tents of the righteous;" Jacob said, though it was more singing than speaking,

"The right hand of the Lord does valiantly.

The right hand of the Lord is exalted;

The right hand of the Lord does valiantly.

I will not die, but live, And tell of the works of the Lord!"

There were shouts of "amen!" and Nathan found himself saying the word for the very first time. His face was starting to hurt from all the smiling, but he just couldn't seem to help it.

He was forgiven!

Nathan was still reeling from that; he truly had no idea he needed forgiving. He'd lived his life trying to be good, to do good, to live on the right side of the law and to be a caring person. But when he'd come to the realization that there truly was a God and that he could no longer deny Him, he'd suddenly been weighed down by the knowledge that he was completely and wholly inadequate in the eyes of a perfect, Holy God.

A Holy God who'd chosen to forgive him, despite his constant denials of His very existence. It was inconceivable.

After a few more back slaps and congratulations, the group settled down, sitting in the chairs around the fire that had started to die down.

"It's funny, isn't it?" Ida asked no one in particular. "Before, the night seemed... evil. But now, not so much."

Nathan grinned at her. "I think that's because before I was evil, but now... not so much." Tammy whacked him with the back of her hand.

"Now that you accepted Jesus, you're not evil at all, silly," she admonished. Nathan shrugged.

"Guess I have a lot to learn." He smiled at his wife. "I won't argue now when you want to read your Bible."

"Hallelujah!" Tammy shouted, shaking her hands in the air and making the others laugh.

They chatted quietly for a while before people started yawning. Nathan glanced heavenward, thinking it had to be well after midnight. Jacob stood and helped Ida to rise, then they said their goodnights and shuffled off.

Martin and Bette were next, though Jim and Juana, along with Debby, Jasmine, and the other woman Nathan couldn't remember the name of, seemed content to stay where they were. Carl and Tammy both yawned at the same time, then giggled and poked each other, saying "Jinx." Nathan knew they'd be next in wanting to head to bed.

Moments later, Tammy stood and tugged Carl up with her. "C'mon," she told the protesting kid, "I know you're as tired as I—"

"Well, now, this is cozy, isn't it Pete?"

The man's voice startled them all and they turned to see a group of men standing just at the edge of the fire's light, which cast eerie shadows on their faces. If Nathan hadn't seen the real thing earlier, he would have sworn the men looked demonic.

But they could be possessed...

He shook that thought away as he rose slowly, watching from his peripherals as Jim, too, stood, along with a few of the women. Even from across the fire, he could see that the newcomers were armed with rifles and shotguns, which they all held, ready to fire.

"Can we help you gentlemen?" Jim asked, with more politeness than Nathan thought he would have been able to muster himself.

One of the men—Nathan realized there were eight of them—stepped closer, a wicked-looking grin on his face.

"Don't suppose you can," he told Jim, then nodded toward Juana standing next to her husband, clinging to his arm. "But your woman there can help us." He looked around at the other females.

"All of them, in fact, will come in... handy." There were snickers from the newcomers at that, then one murmured something. The man who'd spoken grinned as he turned back to them.

"Jay here says the boy will do for him."

Nathan blinked a few times. He knew what the men were implying; it was obvious to everyone, even

Carl, who he saw stiffen next to Tammy at the man's words. Nathan started to reach for the nine-millimeter, but then cursed inwardly when he realized he didn't have it, and his other weapons were in his duffel, too far behind him to be of any use.

Jim must have been thinking along the same lines. "Left my gun back in the tent," he murmured, too low for the others to hear. "Got excited when I heard about you getting saved and ran off without it." Nathan didn't answer; there wasn't any need to. The men were well-armed, and they weren't.

The odds weren't looking good.

Nathan contemplated the options—they could rush the men and hope to overpower them, but that would require everyone being on the same page and there wasn't any way to communicate a plan. If he alone rushed them, that would be suicide.

It was funny, he thought; just an hour or so earlier, he'd been planning that very thing. Now, he found that he didn't want to die. Not at all.

But there was no way he was going to let them take any of the women—or Carl. The thought of that made Nathan shudder. It was bad enough that the men wanted to abuse the women, but a kid? Nathan gritted his teeth against the idea.

Carl—with the nine-millimeter in the back of his pants—was too far away for Nathan to reach. Besides, the weapon's magazine only held ten rounds, one of which had already been fired. It would take some really accurate shooting to make sure all eight men were incapacitated with only nine rounds.

And avoid getting shot—or getting anyone else shot—in the process.

Talk about a rock and a hard place, Nathan thought, a bit hysterically. They were in a no-win situation, an impossible—

"Do not be afraid of them, For I am with you to deliver you..."

Nathan grinned when he heard the voice in his head again. This time, he knew exactly Who it was speaking.

"Okay, Lord, this is all You," he muttered. Jim glanced his way, a slight smile on his face and Nathan wondered if he'd heard God speaking too.

Nathan found himself taking a deep breath, almost as if he were no longer in control of his own body. When he opened his mouth to speak, he knew that was the case.

The Holy Spirit Himself was speaking through him.

"Father in Heaven, Creator of earth above and below, of worlds beyond our imaginings, show Your mighty hand. Reveal Your presence to all here, including those wishing to do evil. Open their eyes that they might see!"

Nathan opened his own eyes then when he heard the gasps. It wasn't just from the newcomers; Jacob and the others had turned and were staring in awe at the area behind Nathan. He turned as well and grinned, not at all surprised by what he saw, though a part of him knew he *should* be. But he knew he was still seeing through the Holy Spirit, who knew exactly what was there.

An army of gigantic angels, all glowing with unearthly fire, stood behind them, ready to defend.

Nathan turned back to see how the men who'd been so sure of themselves when they'd been looking to rape and who knew what else would react. They looked like they were either going to be sick or shake themselves to death. To a one, they all turned and fled.

"Jesus will forgive you!" Nathan yelled out to them. "You just have to repent and turn to Him before it's too late! And soon it will be!"

His announcement was met with silence and Nathan couldn't help but feel a bit disappointed.

Chuckling turned his attention back to the angel army. Zadkiel stepped forward with a grin.

"What?" Nathan asked.

The angel shook his head. "Dude, it sure didn't take you long to change your attitude. From 'there's no such thing as God' to calling on Abba's army and witnessing to your enemy." He reached out and clapped a giant hand on Nathan's shoulder.

"Abba is very happy with you. Good job."

Nathan grinned back at the angel, first for his use of American slang, but mostly because he'd pleased God.

"Well, that isn't going to be the first and last time," Nathan told the angel with surety. "I'm going to tell everyone about the Lord now." He shook his head.

"I wasted too much time. Too much of my life was spent denying the Father and I know I can't make up for that. But I'm gonna spend what's left of my life bringing as many to Heaven with me as I can." Sadness came over him then when he realized how very little time there was left. So very little time left for the world... but even less for him.

Zadkiel smiled down at him. "That's all Abba expects of you." He looked up at the others. "That's all

240

He expects of any of you who call Him Lord... that you spend your remaining days here on earth praising Him and telling those who don't know Yeshua about Him. It's imperative that you move quickly."

"Why is that?" Carl asked. Nathan was impressed that the kid had the gumption to even speak when there were countless flaming angels surrounding them.

If he hadn't been watching the angel before him, Nathan might have missed the flicker of unease that crossed Zadkiel's face. He actually sighed as he looked around at the believers staring at him.

"The Fourth Seal has been broken."

Nathan wasn't sure what that meant, but the Spirit within him shuddered.

"What's that?" one of the women asked. Nathan didn't turn around to see who it was.

Zadkiel started to speak, but Carl interrupted him. "I looked, and behold, an ashen horse; and he who sat on it had the name Death; and Hades was following with him. Authority was given to them over a fourth of the earth, to kill with sword and with famine and with pestilence and by the wild beasts of the earth."

When he'd begun speaking, Nathan had turned to the kid in surprise. Carl snapped his mouth shut, then giggled. "Uh, sorry. Don't know where that came from."

"It came from what you call the Book of Revelation," Zadkiel said. Nathan turned to look at the angel and saw that he was smiling at Carl fondly. "And the Spirit within you revealed it through you." He then made it a point to look at each of the believers.

"Until the end of this time you call the Tribulation, all of you who call on the Name of the Lord will need to lean upon the Holy Spirit for strength and guidance. There will be times when one of us—" he motioned to the flaming army behind him, "—might come to you to help or to deliver a message, but there will be many times when you may find yourselves on your own.

"Just remember the One who walks with you is the One who wrote the story. The Beginning and the End. He is your strength when you're too weak to fight. He is your defender when you have nothing left. Through Him you will have victory."

Zadkiel smiled at them. "Don't forget—in the end, He wins. We all do."

"Children, it is the last hour, and as you have heard that antichrist is coming, so now many antichrists have come. Therefore we know that it is the last hour." 1 John 2:18

It sure feels like we're at the last hour, doesn't it? I believe that is due to the fact that IT IS! We are on the very cusp of the end of this age and the war to end all wars will soon be upon us.

But if you're a believer, you don't need to fear this time. The Lord will guide you, lead you, provide for you, protect you, or welcome you home to His loving arms. How amazing is that?

If you're not a believer, I have to ask: What's stopping you? The Creator of the entire Universe adores you and wants you to come home! He wants all of His prodigals to come to the banquet. All you have to do is head down the road to Him and He'll run to you with open arms!

Here is a simple prayer you can pray:

Dear God in Heaven, I come to You in the name of Jesus. I acknowledge to You that I am a sinner, and I am sorry for my sins and the life that I have lived; I need your forgiveness.

I believe that Your only begotten Son, Jesus Christ, shed His precious blood on the cross at Calvary and died for my sins, and I am now willing to turn from my sin.

You said in the Bible that if we confess the Lord our God and believe in our hearts that God raised Jesus from the dead, we will be saved.

With my heart, I believe that God raised Jesus from the dead. This very moment I accept Jesus Christ

243

as my own personal Savior and according to His Word, right now I am saved. Amen.

If you meant that prayer in your heart, WELCOME TO THE FAMILY!

Book 2, **HIDING,** from the *Saints of Salvation* series:

The world as we knew it has ended.

No surprise there; the Scriptures warned us about this for thousands of years.

And yet... we were shocked.

Unprepared.

Devastated.

Now we're on the run. It's not easy. We have to hide from the others, those with evil on their minds. Sometimes we have to fight against them. Do what it takes to make it through.

Our only hope is to find other people like us. Those who know what's going to happen. Believers. Together, we might stand a chance.

We just have to survive until then.

Coming October 26, 2021. Available on Amazon for pre-order.

<u>Beginning the End</u> Book 1 of The End Series

My name is Nikki. Just a country gal with no real mad skills. But after the global economic collapse, my husband Reg and I found ourselves leading a ragtag group of survivors, those who managed to escape the cities... and the Neos. The Neo Geo Task Force is the new government. The new world order. They were supposed to be the law of the land, the peacekeepers. They were anything but.

<u>Surviving the End</u> Book 2 of The End Series

This time, our present, was the end of the age. Or, at least the slippery downward slope heading toward the end. My name is Nikki and with my husband Reg we tried our best to protect our growing group of survivors. Everything that happened had been foretold in ancient texts, some written long before Christ walked the earth. But even knowing the prophesy didn't completely prepare us for just how difficult those times would be.

<u>Embracing the End</u> Book 3 of The End Series

While the rest of the world was celebrating the establishment of the "new world order," we were struggling just to eat. We fought to live, to exist. We never could have imagined just how bad things would get. But betrayal was our worst enemy. The Lord never left us, though. His promises kept us going, gave us direction. He led us and guided our steps, even when those steps took us right up to the Neos' doorstep. And then we were no longer fighting. We were storming the gates of Hell.

<u>Conquering the End</u> Book 4 of The End Series

The hunt continues. But now the entire world is after us. We are Followers of The Way—believers of the Christ. Our enemy, the Neos, have morphed into something even worse than the demon-possessed Satan minions they were.

Now they rule the world, and their quest is to annihilate anyone who stands in their way. Which means us. We know that Christ wins in the end; we just have to survive until then. We just hope the last day comes quickly, because the earth is going to Hell.

The Releasing Book 1 in the Reign of the Lion Series

The End Series continues with Allie and the Remnants in the Millennial Period. It's been nearly one thousand years since the Tribulation, and it's supposed to be a time of peace. But Allie is up to her eyeballs trying to deal with backtalking Remnants, arrogant angels, a joking Abba and an annoying growing affection for her right-hand man. And of course, there is the small fact that Lucifer is going to be unleashed on the world soon...

The Tempting Book 2 in the Reign of the Lion Series

While Satan oozes his fake charm to gather all those who might turn to the dark side, Allie has her hands full — an unruly team of Remnants, a man who keeps her teeth grinding and hormones raging, a pet bobcat who couldn't keep her nose out of Allie's business, angel warriors who insist on doing things their own way...and, oh yeah, that pesky angel rebellion to deal with.

The Gathering Book 3 in the Reign of the Lion Series

Never in a million years would Allie have ever guessed that she'd be part of Lucifer's tempting of those born in the Millennium. But after being captured by the gorgeous Prince of All Things Slimy, she was not only a part of it... she was the biggest tool in the evil dude's arsenal. By keeping her bound under the paralysis power Allie had come to despise, Lucifer assumed she was completely under his control. Powerless. Helpless. That was his biggest mistake yet.

The Consuming Book 4 in the Reign of the Lion Series

Allie isn't thrilled with her new assignment. It means putting herself in danger of being captured by Lucifer once again. But this time, she won't be a captive--she'll be an example. She'll do her best to follow Abba's wishes, but she knows it's not going to be easy. Witnessing to Lucifer's army is not exactly going to be a church picnic. To top it off, she has the upcoming war with said army on her mind. At best, they'll be able to win the army to Abba's side, to salvation. At worst? Allie's head will become Lucifer's new war helmet.

Road Trip Revival Series, Seniors Road Trip (and by "senior," we mean well-seasoned!)

When you lose everything you have... you might just gain the world. In the Road Trip Revival Series, Jean finds herself just a bit lost after the death of her husband. Suddenly alone—and lonely—she doesn't quite know where her place in the world is. But when she hears a pastor talk about a revival, something changes.

Now she's on a mission from God.

Mama's Heart Book 1 in The Tapestry Series

Misty is shocked to learn she's pregnant, and out of wedlock too. But all things work out, until a fateful day when her entire world is turned upside down. Misty becomes bitter, angry, and questions everything she ever knew about God. But a surprise visit from a stranger helps her put life into perspective and to see God's handiwork in weaving the tapestry of her life.

Unanswered Prayers Book 2 in The Tapestry Series

Steve Tyler is the typical mid-western kid... a little nerdy, very smart, with a great future. Through a series of life-changing events and "unanswered" prayers, Steve turns his back on God and turns to drugs for his comfort. Homeless, friendless and hopeless where every day is a struggle just to survive, Steve finds himself in such a deep valley that the only way up is by taking God's hand.

Here, Hold My Beer Confessions of the Common Sense Challenged Male

Stories that will break your funny bone and keep you in stitches... and you won't have to go to the ER! Humor satire about the dumb things that guys will sometimes do. You know, those decisions that usually start with a trip to the liquor store and end up with a trip to the hospital. If you like to hear those "chill around the fire pit, guzzling six packs and spitting tobacco at the flames" kind of stories, this book is for you!

Made in United States
North Haven, CT
31 January 2023